Growing up so close to the powerful Romano family, twenty-year-old Caterina Russo has always been good buddies with their youngest son, Luciano. How could she predict that being sent to fetch him downstairs for dinner with their families would bring her face-to-face with his latest lover — or worse, that she'd be so suddenly smitten by him? Any such feelings must immediately be quashed, buried too deep to ever threaten her again.

Stellina — Luciano's *little star.* He has always planned to put a ring on Caterina's finger, just not yet. No need to clip his wings at only twenty-five, not even for her. So why does he find himself monitoring her every move, rescuing her from dangerous situations, and instantly enraged if another man so much as looks at her? And what can he possibly say when, in desperation to avoid an arranged marriage, she asks him to marry her?

But *yes* is only the beginning. Having grown up under the harsh rules of mafia families, can either Caterina or Luciano ever learn to trust? Can they possibly overcome the obstacles those same families throw in their way? They'll have to fight for what they want — together.

Stellina
Copyright © 2024 Wie-aam Adams
ISBN: 978-1-4874-4135-7
Cover art by Martine Jardin

Published by eXtasy Books Inc

Look for us online at:
www.eXtasybooks.com

Stellina
The Romano Brothers 2

By

Wie-aam Adams

CHAPTER ONE: CATERINA

I bang on the door.

"Lucian, open up!" I yell out.

Nothing. I groan in frustration.

"Luciano Romano. You better open up right now, or I swear I'll—"

The door flies open, revealing a half-naked Lucian in only a pair of boxer shorts, his top half completely bare. I gulp, staring at his bare chest that's covered in tattoos with random swirls and patterns. He's not nearly as tatted as his two older brothers, but he's still tatted, nonetheless.

He clears his throat, and my head snaps up to his, my cheeks flushing at the realization that I've been caught staring.

Then I look at him properly. The messy bed hair and the lipstick stains on his neck. He looks like someone who just had sex.

I ignore the pang in my chest. Yes, he probably had the best night of his life, fucking some random girl he met at some club while I stayed at home, curled up in bed with a book. But that shouldn't bother me. He's Luciano Romano, after all, and whatever he does and who he does it with shouldn't matter to me. It really shouldn't, but it does, for reasons I don't even want to think about.

He notices me staring at the obvious post-sex signs and opens his mouth to say something, but an incredibly annoying feminine voice butts in.

"Luciano," the voice calls out, so squeaky, it makes me

1

cringe. "Who is it?"

So I was right, after all. I may be inexperienced in that area, but I still know stuff when I see it. I don't read for nothing.

Plastering an obviously fake smile on my face, I tell Lucian, "Your father says to come down for brunch, since you clearly forgot me and my family were coming over today."

Then I turn around to walk away, but he grabs my arm, pulling me back.

"What?" I hate how bitter I sound.

He just stares down at me, his eyebrows furrowed. The way he stares at me, it's like he's trying to figure me out, and I hate it. I hate it when he tries to read me. I'm afraid I'll give too much away.

"What?" I repeat, louder this time.

Then he tips his head back, stepping aside so that the girl he slept with comes into view. She's stark naked. The silk bed-sheets are barely covering her body. She's pretty, blonde and blue-eyed. The complete opposite of me.

"Get rid of her for me," he says instead of asking. I glare at him. Is he seriously asking me to get rid of his one-night stand for him? How cruel can one person be?

"What do I look like to you?" I snap, pulling my arm out of his hold. Then I stomp away before he can try and reach for me again. I make my way down the stairs to the dining room where our families are sitting.

They all turn to me when I reach the table.

"He's coming," is all I say before taking a seat next to my mother. I try not to think about Lucian and his conquest of the previous night as we wait. Of course, they won't start eating without him.

"Are you okay?" my sister, Alba, whispers to me. I resist the urge to sigh. Of course I can hide my emotions from everyone else, but she notices. Sometimes I hate how close we are and how well she knows me. She's only one year older than me, twenty-one years old, and I guess that's why we get along better than with our eldest sister, Viola, who's ten years older than me and nine years older than Alba.

"I'm okay," I lie, hoping that even if she sees through it, she'll let it go.

Then, a few minutes later, Lucian comes strolling into the dining room, probably after saying goodbye to his . . . whatever that girl was.

He's cleaned himself up quickly, now dressed in a pair of black trousers and a crisp white shirt that he's rolled up at the forearms. I hate to admit it, but he looks really handsome all cleaned up. Although his dark hair is as messy as always, like he never bothers to tame those thick tresses, and his bright blue eyes are filled with mischief, like he's a cheeky little child, even at the age of twenty-five.

He stops right behind my chair. I freeze when I feel his presence behind me, the hairs on the back of my neck standing up in anticipation. I resist the urge to groan. What will he do *now*?

Then he turns to Alba and says quite bluntly, "Move."

"What?" Poor Alba blinks in confusion.

"I said move," he says, his voice snappy and impatient.

"Honey, come sit on my other side," our mother says when Alba has no idea what to do. I roll my eyes. Of course Lucian gets his way. Even in my family, the Russo family, he's treated like royalty, like better than their own children.

Alba rises up from her seat and hurries to the one on the left of our mother, her cheeks red in embarrassment.

"Luciano, was that really necessary?" Lucian's father, Gio Romano, asks, his tone telling us that he's tired.

Lucian merely grins, sitting down next to me. His father hardly seems bothered by his blatant disrespect, almost as if he's used to it by now. Of course. Lucian is the baby of the family, and so he's spoiled. People think the same of me, even though that's the furthest from the truth. "Well, dig in, every-one."

Everyone starts eating while I just sit there, my appetite having left me the moment I saw Lucian emerge from his bedroom in *that* state.

Then suddenly Lucian scoots closer to me, moving the whole chair to me. I turn to him with questioning eyes.

"Are you not going to eat?" he whispers to me so that only I can hear him.

"I'm not hungry," I tell him, looking away from him.

"Did you eat yet today?" he asks, and I shake my head. My mother told us to not eat anything today, not even a bread crumb, because we would be brunching here, and we didn't want to be full and disrespect the Romano family by not even eating anything. Although, that's exactly what's happening here with me, albeit for a different reason.

Lucian picks up a croissant and holds it in front of my mouth. I furrow my eyebrows at him. *What's he doing?*

"Eat," he simply says.

I shake my head.

"It wasn't a request, *stellina*."

There it is. That stupid nickname. It means *my star* in Italian. When I was younger, like a fool, I thought it meant something, that maybe *I* meant something to him, but boy, was I wrong. I never made the mistake of falling for it again.

"I'm not eating." I huff like a little child.

"Yes. You. Will," he says, holding the croissant closer to my mouth.

I purse my lips closed when I realise that he might just stuff it in my mouth if I defy him any longer.

"Caterina, baby, be a good girl and eat the croissant," he murmurs into my ear. My entire body tenses up. But like I'm not in control of my own limbs, I take the croissant from him and take a bite out of it. He reaches up and rubs his hand down the back of my head. "Good girl."

My entire body heats up at his words.

Oh, lord, I think I may have a praise kink.

For him.

For Luciano Romano.

Fuck.

CHAPTER TWO: LUCIANO

Such a pretty little baby.

She has fire in her, defiance, but when I call her that, so sweetly and praise her, it's like she melts for me completely.

Caterina Russo. The bane of my existence.

I hadn't expected to see her at my bedroom door today. If I had, I would've gotten rid of Christy, or Anna, or whatever her name was, a long time ago. I would've never let Caterina see that. But she did. And fuck, did she glare at me.

She looked so angry, and then, like a complete stupid dick, I asked her to get rid of the girl for me. That was the last straw. She stared at me like she thoroughly despised me before stomping off. Fuck, it may be messed up, but seeing that fiery look in her eyes . . . made me hard. So fucking hard. All for her. Just for her.

I look up from *stellina* to find her mother staring at us with narrowed eyes, but when I catch her, she immediately looks down. Of course she would. Despite the Russos being one of the wealthiest families in Italy, their power is still nothing compared to ours, the Romanos.

We're the Italian mafia family, after all.

I bring my attention back to *her*.

"Was that nice?" I ask her, and she nods, albeit reluctantly. "Want another one?"

She turns her head to mine, and fuck, she's beautiful.

With those innocent doe brown eyes, she can bring any man to his knees.

"Yes, please," she whispers, her voice so soft I barely catch it. But I do, and so I grab another croissant and hand it to her. She doesn't protest this time. She just eats happily.

I spend the rest of the brunch just watching her. Unlike other girls, she isn't shy about stuffing her face if she's hungry. In fact, she asks me to pass her something at least three more times, and when she's full, it's obvious on her face.

I stare down at her, my focus on the hand that splays over her stomach. Her left hand. It's completely bare, not a ring in sight, and I keep my eyes on her empty ring finger. One day. One day, I'll put a ring on that finger.

My infatuation with Caterina Russo is no secret in my family, and the only reason why my father doesn't protest the idea is because of what family she comes from. I still remember my older brother, Alessandro, falling in love with a commoner, and ultimately, he lost his title, and it was given to our eldest brother, Dante. Unlike them, I'm not interested in being the Don. I'm fine just the way I am, and besides, unless Dante fucks up or dies, I'll never get the title, seeing as I'm the youngest. Father says I'm still too wet behind the ears to be Don. Not that I care. I'm perfectly fine with the way things are right now.

Stellina taps me on the shoulder, bringing my attention back to her.

"Yes, *stellina*?" I love the way she blushes when I call her that. *Stellina*, my star. It's fitting because that's exactly what she is and what she means to me. I'd give my life for this woman. Without a single doubt.

"Can I have some orange juice?" she whispers to me, and I smile. She's never shy with anyone, always being bold and making her opinions heard, but right now, she's relying solely on me. I'm the only one she's talking to, the only one she's looking at. I love that. I don't want her looking at any other man but me. Not even my father. Because I know very well what a perverted bastard he can be sometimes.

Pouring a little orange juice into a glass, I hand it to Caterina, who takes it willingly and hums as she takes long sips of it. I can't stop myself from reaching out and cupping the back of her head. She freezes momentarily but doesn't push me away.

Seriously, how can this girl not see how absolutely enamoured I am by her? I think she's the only one who doesn't know. I know her catching me this morning wasn't a good look, but still. Surely, she should have some sense of what I feel for her? I can't be more obvious.

When brunch is over, I pull Caterina away from our families and up the stairs.

"Where are we going?" she asks, but she doesn't protest, just lets me drag her with me. I stop in front of my bedroom, and she grimaces. "I'm not going in there."

I smile at her.

"What? You can't tell me that the remnants of your night with that girl aren't still there," she says, her voice bold, but her lips still forming a pout, like she's sulking.

"I had the cleaner clean up my room while we were downstairs," I inform her, but she still narrows her eyes at me. Then I wrap my arm around her waist and pull her flush against me. She lets out a soft gasp. "Why? Is there another reason why you won't go in there?"

She glares up at me.

"Come on, baby," I say, leaning down. "Don't be like that."

There's barely an inch between our faces, and my eyes flicker down to her lips. That pout, I want to kiss it away.

"Be like what?" she challenges. "I don't want to go in there, so I won't." She huffs as if to make her point.

"I just wanted you to help me pack," I give in and say. Her eyebrows raise.

"Pack?" I might be imagining it, but she sounds a little sad. "Are you going somewhere?"

I nod.

"I'm moving out."

"Where?" she blurts out, her curiosity getting the better of her.

I smile. "Just an apartment in the city," I answer. Then I smirk. "Why? Were you scared that you'd never see me again?"

"Yes," she shocks me by saying. Then she wraps her arms around my lower back. "You may be a dick, but you can't go anywhere too far away from me. After all, you're my only friend."

"Aw, you consider me your friend?" I tease.

"Don't ruin it, Lucian," she snaps, and I smile, pulling her impossibly closer with both arms. She seems to be more comfortable in my arms now, considering how she grips my shirt in between her fingers.

"I'm not going anywhere, *stellina*," I murmur, grazing her nose with my own. "I'd never leave you."

And it's true. I'd never leave her.

Not even in death.

Chapter Three: Caterina

"Miss Russo, you really shouldn't do this."

I shrug off the words of my personal maid, Mary.

Yes, she may be right. Yes, this may be stupid. But this is something I want to do.

It's no fair that others get to have fun, but I can't. Yes, I'm the youngest daughter of the Russo family, but still. I need some sort of freedom myself. Viola goes out every other night with her friends, and although Alba prefers to stay home, she still has that choice. Whereas me, I don't.

"Then, shall I call Mr Romano?" Mary offers.

I sigh, shaking my head.

The Mr Romano she's talking about is none other than Lucian, and instead of supporting me in my decision, he'd convince me to stay home like the good girl I am. Like the good girl I've always been. In fact, he'd lock me up if he could. For what reason, I have no idea.

"I'm going on my own," I announce, ignoring the way Mary cringes. I'm a big girl now. I'm almost twenty-one, yes, only in a year, but I'm basically an adult now. No, I'm an adult.

"Then, Miss. Russo . . ." Mary trails off as she hesitates. I raise an eyebrow at her. "I'll come with you."

"You'll get in trouble," I point out, although that's useless because the moment she lets me out those doors, she's in trouble.

"I'd rather be there with you than worry about you here," she says, and although I want to protest, wanting that taste of freedom, I find myself nodding in agreement. With her there, it won't be so bad. She isn't as restricting as everyone else.

She breathes out in relief.

"Now, how about you help me pick out an outfit?" I tell her, and she nods, stepping forward and scanning my closet with narrowed eyes.

"Is there a specific theme you're going for here, Miss. Russo?" she asks.

Sexy might be a bit dangerous, especially since I'm planning on just having some fun, not ending up in bed with a stranger, but still. I find myself faltering. I've never considered myself sexy, especially since I'm always wearing clothes that cover up everything, as per my father's instructions. He doesn't even know of the little sexy options I have in my closet, and I've never had an opportunity to show them off, but this might be the right time.

"Sexy," I go with, and she nods, albeit reluctantly. Then she sticks her hand into my closet and comes out with a little black sparkly number. It's skin-tight, off-the-shoulder, and really short. Mary's eyes widen when she examines the dress, but I grab it from her before she can put it back.

"M-miss Russo—"

"Thank you," I say with a smile, cutting her off. "Grab something from my closet for yourself. You can't go to a club wearing your work clothes."

Then I disappear into the bathroom to change. When I'm done and emerge from the bathroom in the dress, Mary's eyes become wide. I'm happy to see her wearing a dress of mine, one a lot less revealing than mine, but still. She looks cute.

"How do I look?" I ask, giving her a little twirl. I did minimalistic makeup to go with the dress but went a little bold with a winged liner. As for my hair, I left it down in its natural waves. I think I look good.

"Miss Russo, you look . . . exactly how you intended to,"

she says, awkwardly skipping over the use of the word sexy.

I smile, satisfied.

"Then we can go," I say, grabbing a matching black purse and walking out the door.

We catch a taxicab to a club downtown. I don't know its name and apparently, it's not that popular. It's a good thing for me, though, because there's no risk of me running into people who know my family.

When we arrive, the name *The Dungeon* stares down at me. The Dungeon . . . I'm not sure how fitting that is. Kind of sounds like an illegal underground fighting ring.

Shrugging off my thoughts, I lead Mary down the line, and the bouncer lets us in without an ID check, thank goodness. My name is on my ID card, and even here, down in the dumps, the Russos are known.

Immediately, I'm hit with smoke, causing me to cough.

"Miss Russo —"

"Cat," I interject. "You call me Cat tonight."

She nods, although the distress is evident on her face. I understand why. This place is not what I expected at all. The entire place is covered in smoke, and I can barely see anything. I try to ignore it, though. I made this decision — this choice — and I'm not about to back out, not without a proper try first.

"Are you sure I shouldn't call —"

"I'm sure," I cut in, already knowing what she's going to say. Then, as if on point, my phone dings with a message, and I spot Lucian's name in my notifications. I should probably respond, but just as I'm about to click on the notification, I'm pushed forward by a strong force, and my phone slips from my hand and lands on the floor with a crack.

Great.

I look around, trying to find my phone on the floor, and it's when I'm crawling on the floor that I realise that I've lost Mary. *Oh no.*

I stand up immediately, calling out her name, but I can't even hear myself over the loud music. I try to look around, but all I see is white smoke.

Then, a pair of hands land on my waist from behind, and I'm pulled into a stranger's chest. I freeze.

Why are you freezing, Caterina? Isn't this what you wanted? Come to a club full of strangers and have fun? So why are you hesitating? Dance with him.

And then my body starts moving on its own . . . my mind is still clouded with doubts, though. The stranger starts grinding against my behind, his body moving sensually, but I don't feel anything. I don't feel aroused. Not at all.

Then he spins me around, pressing his hard-on against my stomach. I gasp at the unfamiliar feeling. This . . . I've never experienced this before. I'm not sure I like it, though, not from a stranger.

My mind flashes to Lucian. The way he looks at me, the way his touch feels on my body. Now that sets my nerves and senses alight. Not this. Not this stranger.

I try to pull away from him, but he just pulls me closer, thrusting his hips up against mine. I purse my lips, blinking through sudden tears. I don't want this. Why in the world did I think this was a good idea?

"Let me go," I say, but even I can't hear my own pleading. He just pulls me closer, leaning down so that his mouth is by my neck.

"You sexy little thing," he mutters into my ear. "You little slut."

Tears flow down my face. I'm not a slut. I'm really not. I haven't even had sex yet.

Then suddenly, I'm ripped off him, and I hear the sound of a crack. I'm spun around, hands placed firmly on my arms. I look up through teary eyes, and although I can't see the person, I smell them. *Him.*

I collapse into his arms, willing him to never let me go.

He came for me.
Lucian came for me.

Chapter Four: Luciano

I stare at my phone in anger.

Why the fuck has she not responded to my message? She even left it unread. What's she doing that she can't even open my message?

"Trouble in paradise?"

I look up with an instant glare, recognizing the voice.

My eldest brother, Dante, stares at me with amusement in his eyes.

"Fuck off," I snap, looking back at my phone, willing for a notification to pop up, willing for her to message me.

Dante and I have never had a good relationship. In fact, he doesn't get along with me or Sandro. And whose fault is it? It can only be his, of course. He's a grade-A dick. He has a rotten personality, and personally, he hates Sandro and me for having meaningful relationships with women. He's a sick bastard who treats women like toys created only for his enjoyment.

A part of me feels sorry for him, though, because even after everything, he's still my big brother, and I want him to be happy. He says sleeping with a different woman every night pleases him, but that's not what I want for him. I want him to be *happy*, truly happy. Too bad he doesn't believe in love, though. If he would just give it a chance, he'd see that there's happiness worth chasing.

Ironically, the woman in my life is the cause of my irritation right now. Why the fuck is she not replying?

Then suddenly, my phone starts ringing, and my momentary hope leaves me when I see that it's an unknown number.

I ignore the call.

"You do something that has unknown numbers calling you?" Dante asks, and I shake my head.

See? Even if he acts like a dick ninety-nine per cent of the time, I believe he does care, even just a little. It makes me think that maybe there's hope for him after all.

Then the number calls again. I decline the call.

"So what brings you home?" I ask, leaning back in my chair. He shrugs.

"And you? I thought you moved out," he points out.

"I just came to get a few last things," I say.

"Liar." He sees right through me. "The Russos live a few houses down, and you were hoping you'd run into that little princess of yours."

"Don't talk about her," I snap. He may be my brother, but I hate other men talking about her. Him being single with a questionable taste in younger girls ticks me off. He raises his hands in defence.

"She's not my type," he says defensively. "Besides, I don't want my younger brother's sloppy seconds."

I'm about to say something when the same unknown number calls again. I answer with a huff.

"What the fuck do you want?" I snap into the call.

"*M-Mr Romano,*" an oddly familiar voice stammers into the call.

"Who is this?" I ask.

"It's Mary. I-I'm sorry, Mr Romano. Miss. Russo gave me your phone number for emergencies . . ."

Miss Russo? *Stellina.*

"What is it? Has something happened to Caterina?" I question, rushing to my feet. Dante quirks an eyebrow at me.

"*Miss Russo . . .*" She trails off with a choked sob.

"Where are you?" I ask. She just sobs. "Tell me where the fuck you are right now!"

"*The Dungeon*," she silently whispers, as if she's waiting for me to explode.

"I'm coming," I tell her before I hang up.

"What's going on?" Dante asks me.

"It's Caterina. She's at *The Dungeon*."

His eyes widen a fraction.

"I'll drive you," he says, leaving no room for protest, not that I was going to. I'm not in the right state of mind to drive right now.

We rush to Dante's car and get in, the engine roaring as he speeds off.

The Dungeon. What was she thinking? *Fuck.*

In no time, we're pulling up to *The Dungeon,* and I'm out of the car immediately, rushing past the bouncer, who immediately recognizes me and lets me in without a word. The moment I enter, I'm engulfed by smoke.

Fuck, I can't see a thing.

Closing my eyes, I focus on my hearing. Come on, let me hear you, *stellina.*

Then I hear it.

"Let me go." I hear her sweet voice plead. My eyes snap open. That bastard. He's dead.

I stomp towards the source, my body colliding with a soft one. When the scent of vanilla and apples enters my senses, I know. It's her.

I rip her away from the stranger before my fist makes contact with his jaw.

I want to kill him for touching her, but she collapses in my arms before I can make another move. She sniffles, burying her face in my chest. I run my hand down the back of her head, wrapping my free arm around her waist.

"It's okay," I murmur. "I'm here now, *stellina.*"

The smoke slowly dissipates, and then I see her. When I do,

my blood boils. What the fuck is she wearing? She's barely covered.

Even I've never seen her this exposed before. I thank the heavens, if they do exist, that the smoke prevented other men from seeing her, and I drape my jacket around her. A hand lands on my shoulder, and my head snaps around, my eyes in a fierce glare. My glare ceases when I see that it's only Dante.

"Is she okay?" he asks, not even glancing at the woman cradled in my arms. I nod. "Let's go. I'll take you home."

"To my place," I insist as we walk to his car. He merely nods.

I sit in the backseat, pulling Caterina onto my lap. She curls into a little ball in my arms, her breathing finally becoming steady.

"What happened to her personal maid?" I ask Dante.

"I sent her home in a taxicab. What happens with her next is none of my business."

Dante drives to my apartment in the city, pulling up in front of the building. I hesitate, turning to my brother.

"Thank you . . . brother," I awkwardly say. He's never done anything for me before, and so as much as this has been a good development on his part, I'm still not sure how to re-act. This is also the first time I've called him brother in *years*. Not since I was little and idolized him. Not since I found out what kind of person he *really* is. Could I have been wrong, though? Is there really a person underneath that tough exte-rior?

"You owe me," he playfully says, although the awkward-ness in him is evident, as well. Good, I'm not the only one.

I bid him goodbye before getting out of the car with *stellina* in my arms. I walk into the building and head to the elevator. It takes me to the 30th floor. I had the chance and the money to get the apartment on the top floor, the penthouse, but I said no. I wanted something more cozy, more homely, for me . . . and Caterina.

I had a feeling she would appreciate that.

I unlock my apartment door with my fingerprint before pushing open the door and walking inside. The apartment isn't as luxurious as Dante, Sandro's, or my family house, for that matter, but it's quite comfortable to live in. It's also perfect to build a family in. A small little family of my own. The thought makes me excited.

I carry *stellina* to the couch and sit down on it with her back on my lap.

"You sleeping?" I softly ask. She moans, snuggling deeper into my touch. "Do you want to talk about what happened tonight?" Another moan. "What do you need, *stellina*?"

"Just you," she finally speaks. "Just . . . hold me, please."

"I *am* holding you," I tell her, my grip instinctively tightening around her. "I won't let you go until you ask."

She hums in satisfaction.

I don't know how long we just sit here, and just as I'm convinced that she's asleep, she opens her eyes and sits up. She keeps her arms around me, though, as do I to her.

"What's on your mind?" I ask, noticing how stuck she seems in her head.

"Nothing." She shrugs, but I send her a stern look that has her continuing. "I'm just thinking about . . . how stupid I feel."

"Why do you feel stupid?"

"Because of what I did tonight," she says with a sigh. "I should've known better. I should've just stayed home. Or I should've just called you. I just . . . I wanted some freedom, some independence. I had no idea things would go so wrong."

I cup the side of her face in my hand.

"It's okay," I assure her. "Yes, you did a stupid thing, but that's how we learn."

She stares at me through glassy eyes. If I'm being honest, if it wasn't her, if it was someone else, I'd be pissed. But how can I be angry at *her* when she looks at me like this?

"Did you learn something tonight? Are you going to do that again?" I ask her, my tone serious. She shakes her head.

"Never again," she promises. I smile, placing a soft kiss on her forehead.

"Good girl," I praise, and as if in instinct, she blushes. I know she loves it when I praise her. A praise kink, maybe? Anyway, it's because I know she loves it that I keep on doing it, and I'll never stop.

"You know . . ." She suddenly looks shy, playing with her fingers. "Instead of my forehead, my lips are much closer, you know."

My eyes widen. Is she telling me to kiss her . . . on the lips?

She must be drunk. No sober Caterina Russo would ever ask me, Luciano Romano, to kiss her. Especially not there. She's too prideful.

"Come on. It's time for bed," I tell her, ignoring the way her face falls at my words. I get up with her in my arms and carry her to the guest bedroom. I can't have her in my bed tonight. It'll be too tempting. Besides, I don't want the first time we share a bed to be while she's drunk and when she probably won't even remember.

"Lucian," she calls out softly after I have tucked her in bed.

"Yes, baby?"

"Can you lay with me?"

Yep, she's definitely drunk. She might even be hammered, to be honest.

"Go to sleep, *stellina*," I tell her, placing yet another kiss to her forehead. "I'll see you in the morning. Goodnight."

And then I'm out the door.

CHAPTER FIVE: CATERINA

I wake up grumpy.

Why, you might ask? Well, I basically offered myself up on a silver platter to Lucian last night, well, my lips at least, and he didn't even think twice about rejecting me. The jerk.

That was the first and last time I'll ever offer him any part of me because clearly he doesn't want me like that.

Suddenly my mood deflates when I think about it. Wow. He must not have been happy to deal with me last night. He must have found me to be such a burden. That's the last thing I wanted. To be a burden to him. To anyone.

I'm pouting when the door opens, and Lucian peeks inside. He grins when he sees that I'm awake before coming inside.

I try not to ogle his bare chest. He's merely in a pair of low-rise grey sweats, and his chest is completely bare and shining with what I assume is sweat. He must have been working out.

"Hey, sleepy head," he greets, lingering at the door. I must have made him really uncomfortable last night. "I left some water and pain relievers on the bedside table for you."

I furrow my eyebrows, staring at what is indeed water and a couple of tablets. Why did he leave this here for me?

The realization dawns on me. He must have thought I was drunk last night. Is that why . . . why he wouldn't kiss or lay with me last night? Because he didn't want to take advantage of me? The thought has hope rising within me.

Why, you might ask. Well, after last night, I realized something. I need Lucian in my life, and not only because he saved me last night. But it was because of how careful and gentle he was with me, and because of how he took care of me and listened to me cry and assured me that I wasn't stupid. I just made a stupid decision. It was at that moment that I decided I want him in my life, whether it be as my friend or even as . . . my lover.

The thought of Luciano Romano being my lover has my entire body flushing with heat, especially as he stands bare-chested in front of me.

I've never thought about him like that before, but there's no doubt how attractive he is. How attracted *I* am to him. Not doing anything about it is almost suffocating.

"I'm going to take a quick shower, and then we can have breakfast," he says and disappears out the door before I can even say anything. Is this awkward for him, considering how I basically threw myself at him last night? It must be that. Gosh, I feel so embarrassed.

I don't know how long I sit there on the bed, contemplating my next move before he comes walking back into the room, fully dressed, in a new pair of black sweats and a plain white shirt that has the first few buttons unbuttoned.

He's wearing a single silver chain around his neck, and something about it is just . . . so attractive.

"You haven't moved?"

I shake my head, tugging at the material of my dress.

"It's uncomfortable," I tell him. It's a miracle I slept at all last night with this on.

"Come on." He beckons me forward, and as if I can't control my own limbs, I find myself crawling on the bed to him. "Let me help you."

I turn around on the bed, pulling my hair to one side. He places his fingers on the zip and starts pulling it down. My breath hitches when more and more of my back gets revealed to him, and I remember something very important.

I'm not wearing a bra.

He notices as well, inhaling sharply. I immediately wrap my arms around my chest, and he resumes pulling the zipper down. It zips all the way down my back, only stopping at the band of my panties. I wanted to feel sexy both on top and underneath, so I'd put on a pair of black lacy panties that I bought in secret. And now Lucian is seeing it.

He reaches over my shoulders and starts pulling the fabric down. This was not supposed to go this far. After he undid the zipper, I can handle the rest on my own, but he's continuing to *help*, and I'm not stopping him.

When the dress reaches the top of my breasts, he murmurs a husky, "Let go, *stellina*."

And I do. I really do, my arms falling to my sides. The dress falls completely, bunching at my waist. He's standing behind me, so he can't see my bare chest, but I still feel so exposed, my entire back on display for him.

"Lift," he silently commands, tapping my hip. I lift my hips and let him pull the dress down my legs and off me completely. Now I'm half-naked, more than half actually, in front of him. "Would you like a shirt?"

I nod shakily. He slips his shirt off his body and drapes it over me. I hurriedly fasten the buttons, breathing out in relief when I'm covered, well, for the most part. At least I'm not flashing him.

Slowly, I twist around on the bed and face him. My eyes are level with his crotch, and the bulge is *very* obvious. Oh lord. Lucian is turned on. By me.

Then he places a finger under my chin, lifting my head up so that I'm looking at his face instead.

"Shall we get breakfast?" he suddenly asks with a smile.

Gulping, I nod, letting him grab my hand and help me off the bed. The shirt reaches just above my knees, thankfully. He leads me out of the room and down a short hallway to the kitchen.

Considering what kind of man he is, his apartment is impressive and surprisingly cosy.

He leads me to a kitchen island where there are many different dishes placed on top. I sit down on a bar stool, and he sits down next to me, grabbing a croissant and holding it out to me. I take it, biting into it happily. The butter melts in my mouth, and I moan in delight.

"You have a really nice place," I comment, looking around it. Just adjacent to the kitchen is a living room with a balcony on the side and . . . my eyes light up. "Is that a hot tub?"

Lucian nods, smiling at my excitement.

"Can I dip my toes in there later?" I practically beg. Even in my family house where there's practically everything, there's one thing we don't have. A hot tub.

"Are you still going to be here later?"

My face falls. Oh, right. I didn't even consider that he didn't want me around for much longer. He probably has things he needs and wants to do, and I'll just be in the way.

"Right," I say, forcing out a chuckle. Concern creases his brows, and he places his hand on my bare thigh.

"I was just kidding, *stellina*," he says with a frown. "Did I really hurt your feelings?"

I shake my head but look away from him.

"*Stellina*," he calls out, his voice stern. "Baby, look at me."

Finally, I turn back to him.

"I'm sorry. I was just teasing you. I didn't mean to hurt you," he says, his eyes begging me now for forgiveness. I don't say anything for a few moments, and his frown deepens.

"So I can try out the hot tub?" I ask. He blinks in confusion before it dawns on him, and he breaks out into a smile.

"Of course," he says, squeezing my thigh. I suck in a breath. "Everything that's here, you have access to. Nothing is off limits to you."

"Why?" I can't help but ask. "Why me?"

He stares at me for the longest time, a certain look in his eyes. And then he says the simplest words that carry the most meaning.

"Because it's you."

Chapter Six: Caterina

"Can I borrow a shirt and maybe some swim trunks?"

I returned to the guest bedroom after breakfast and realized that I have nothing to wear to the hot tub. All I have is my dress and my underwear, and there's no way I'm going topless in front of Lucian.

"Just wear what you have on now, and I'll give you some clothes to wear after," he calls back. I look down at myself. Panties, yes. Shirt, yes. Bra, no. This may be very dangerous, getting into a hot tub in a white shirt that will definitely stick to my skin once wet.

I shouldn't risk it. I really shouldn't, but do I have any other choice? The answer is simple. No.

Sighing in defeat, I walk out of the room and meet Lucian in the living room. Surprisingly, he's in a pair of swim trunks with his chest bare.

"You're going in with me?" I blurt out. He quirks a brow at me.

"Do you not want me to?" he asks.

"I-it's not that. It's just . . ." I might flash you if you get in there with me.

"Then it's settled. I'm joining you," he says, leaving no room for protest.

Pursing my lips, I follow him to the hot tub on the balcony. He gets in first before turning and holding a hand out to me.

"Come on. The water's nice and warm," he says, offering me an assuring smile. I take his hand and let him pull me into the tub. The moment my skin touches the warm water, I hum in satisfaction. Lucian pulls me onto the bench and lets me sit next to him on it. I was really hoping not to get wet above the chest area, but the moment I sit down, the water flows up all the way to the swell of my breasts.

Great. I'll just have to ask him to look away when I get out.

Closing my eyes, I lean back against the edge of the tub.

"Do you like it?" I hear Lucian ask, and I hum, a smile on my face.

"I'm glad."

Then the water moves, and when I finally decide to open my eyes, Lucian is right next to me. I jump a little, startled. He hardly seems affected, though, staring off into nowhere over the balcony railing.

I take this moment to look at him, *properly*. Ever since we met when we were merely children, I've never *really looked* at him. In my eyes, even now, he's still that cute little boy with a cheeky grin and hair that sticks up in all directions. But somehow, that's changed in a single moment. Now that I'm really looking at him, as a man and not just a kid anymore, I realize just how much he's changed.

Gone are those thin limbs, replaced by muscular arms and thick thighs. Gone is that shortness. He's so tall now at over 6ft. At least 6'1. He's not as tall as his brothers, but he's always been the smallest since we were little.

But some things have stayed the same. The mischievous way his blue eyes sparkle. That cheeky grin on his lips. The way he doesn't bother to tame his hair, although it's much more effortless now, compared to the way it looked when he was a kid.

No. This is no kid. This is a man. And that's obvious to me now.

Then suddenly, his head snaps to mine, my eyes widening when I realize that I've been caught staring.

"Why are you looking at me like that?" he asks.

I shrug. "Just . . . realized you're no longer that snot-nosed kid anymore," I say, avoiding his eyes.

"I stopped being that kid a long time ago, Caterina," he says, his voice serious. The use of my real name and not the nickname has my breath hitching. "Did you only notice now?"

Shamefully, I nod. I don't know why it took me so long when he's clearly no longer a kid. He hasn't been for *many* years.

Then he leans forward, his mouth a breath away from mine.

"And now? What do you think of me now that you no longer see me in that way?" he questions.

How do I see him?

"Not . . . sure," I admit, looking down. My feelings are confusing. One moment I hate him with everything in me, like that morning I caught him with that girl. Then, the next moment, I'm looking for him, and I need him. It's just all so back and forth that I don't even know what it is *I'm* feeling.

He cups my cheek in his hand, causing me to look up at him.

"Then, do you want to know what I think of you?" he asks, but I shake my head, my eyes instinctively going shut. I don't want to know. I really don't.

Why? Because I'm scared. I don't even know what I want to hear from him, but I'm scared that I'll hear the opposite of it, and I'll get hurt. When it comes to him, I can get hurt easily. So I have to protect myself.

"Do you want me to take you home?" he offers, sensing the change in me. I look up at him. His eyes are soft and understanding. I've never seen him look like this before. I didn't think he was capable of it.

Then I nod my head. I think it's best for me to just leave now. For myself.

He nods and then gets out of the tub. I hate ruining the mood, but it just . . . happened. It's not like I did it on purpose. I just hope he's not hurt.

He hands me a towel to cover myself before I can even ask, and I wrap it around myself, thanking him. He doesn't say anything in response, just disappearing into the apartment.

I sigh. He's hurt.

How do I fix it? Can I even fix it? When I don't even know why he's hurt?

He returns to the living room, tossing me a shirt and a pair of shorts.

"Change into that, and we can get going," he says, his eyes cold.

Yep, I ruined things.

CHAPTER SEVEN: CATERINA

When I get home, I look for Mary.

But I can't find her anywhere. She's nowhere in the house. Lucian told me that his brother sent her here in a taxicab. Which means that she should be here.

"Caterina," a voice calls out, and I turn around to find that it's my father.

"Papa," I greet.

"Where have you been?" he immediately demands, his eyes narrowing at my clothes. "And whose clothes are those?"

His tone is slowly becoming angrier as the seconds pass. I know exactly what it looks like.

"I went out with Lucian, and it was late, so I ended up spending the night at his place," I tell my father, only telling part of the truth. "And these clothes are his. I didn't have anything clean to put on."

His eyes narrow even further.

"Why didn't you tell me beforehand? You know you're not allowed out," he tells me.

"But I was with Lucian," I say in response.

"It doesn't matter who you were with," Father snaps. "I expect you to tell me everything."

I purse my lips, swallowing my feelings at what he just said.

"Do you know where Mary is?" I ask instead. He scoffs.

"That useless maid? She left the premises without permission, so I left her in the basement without food and water as punishment."

"Father, that's so cruel!" I yell out.

"Then she shouldn't have broken the rules," he points out before walking away, ending the conversation with him having the last word. It's because he knows how things would have gone if he stayed. I would have made a scene or *thrown a tantrum,* as he likes to say, and there's nothing he hates more than that.

I immediately head over to the basement on my way to Mary. In the basement, there are multiple torture rooms along with a few cells. In the first cell, Mary sits, her ankles chained to the wall.

"Mary!" I gasp. Her head snaps to mine, and almost immediately, her eyes tear up.

"Miss Russo!" she exclaims and attempts to come to the cell gates, but she's pulled back by the chains.

"It's okay. Just stay there," I tell her. She nods, her lips trembling. I sink down in front of the cell gate, wrapping my hands around the bars. "Are you okay? I'm sorry. I'm so sorry, Mary. This is all my fault."

She shakes her head. "I made that decision on my own, and I didn't go with you without considering the consequences. I knew what I was getting myself into, but I did it anyway."

"Why? Why would you do that?" I exclaim.

She smiles sadly. "Because after being here for so many years, the only thing that made it bearable was you, Miss Russo. I would do anything for you," she says through tears.

"I'm going to get you out of here. I promise," I tell her.

She shakes her head. "Sir Russo said that he would let me go tomorrow," she informs me. "I can hold on until then."

"What about food? You must be starving."

"No. I've gone much longer without food before. This is nothing," she says, and that only breaks my heart even further.

"No, you shouldn't have to go through this again," I say, shaking my head. "Things were supposed to be different here."

"They are," she protests. "Before, I had no one. Here, I have you, Miss Russo, and the care you've shown me is more than enough for me to do anything for you."

"I don't want to cause you more hurt," I say with a frown. She smiles.

"I'm not hurt. Not anymore."

Something in me tells me to believe her. And so I nod, standing back up.

"I'll be back later," I tell her, my tone telling her that there's no room for her to protest, and so she just nods. Her smile is so sincere, like this is all worth it. Like I've given her the world. When she's out of here, I won't put her or her safety in jeopardy again.

From now on, I'll be the one to protect her.

Father let Mary go the next day.

At least that's one thing I can count on him for. Keeping his promises.

Despite her protests, I keep Mary in my room, feeding her whatever she wants and letting her sleep in my bed. When she's asleep, I walk downstairs to make myself something to eat. After everything that happened, I haven't had an appetite, but now that Mary's back safe, I can eat in peace and relax.

"Honey," a voice calls out. I turn around with a smile.

"Mama," I greet, letting her pull me into a hug.

My mother is the only one I get along with in this house. Well, besides Alba and Mary. Without the three of them here, my life would be a nightmare.

"I heard you slept out," Mother says.

I internally sigh. Why does this have to be the topic of our conversation? Literally, anything else is welcome.

"Yeah." I shrug.

"With Luciano?" Mother asks, and I nod. Then she sighs. "You two . . . didn't do anything, did you?"

My eyes widen and I shake my head. Yes, he saw me very revealed, but he didn't touch me with any sexual intentions, even if I wanted him to.

"Why are you asking though? Don't you like Lucian?" I can't help but ask her. My mother's always been silent when it comes to Lucian, and before, I thought it was because of how powerful his family is, but now I'm starting to think that she just really doesn't like him. Which is strange because, as far as I know, he hasn't done anything that might've caused her to take offence.

"I don't have a problem with Luciano," Mother says, but she doesn't answer my question. "It's just . . . it's complicated."

"What's complicated?" I ask.

Mother sighs. "You've come of age, Caterina."

Come of age? Age of what . . .

The realization dawns on me.

Marriage.

I'm at the age to get married.

"I didn't want to say anything, but . . . your father has some candidates to become your husband."

Rage fills me. "What the hell?" I exclaim, visibly startling my mother. "This is my life. What makes father think he has a say in who I marry?"

"He's just trying to find the most suitable spouse for you," Mother defends him, and I hate it. I want her to be on my side. I thought she was. "It's all so that you're secured for the future. So that you're protected."

"And he doesn't trust that I can find a man like that myself?" I question.

Mother falters, the truth written all over her face. No way is this happening.

Just yesterday, I was a fifteen-year-old sheltered daughter. Now I'm about to be forced into a marriage with a man I don't know and with so much power that he's probably twice my age.

I shiver at the thought.

Then, a light bulb goes on in my brain.

"Mother, what if I find a suitable spouse myself?" I ask, and her eyebrows furrow in questioning. "It doesn't matter who he is, as long as Father approves, correct?"

"Yes, but—"

"Then it's settled." I cut her off with a determined look on my face.

I'm going to ask Lucian to marry me.

CHAPTER EIGHT: CATERINA

I bang on Lucian's apartment door.
Lucian, come on. Open up!

"Look, I know you're mad at me, but please open up. It's urgent." I plead through the door. Then the door flies open, and it's not Lucian I see. Instead, I come face to face with his mother.

"Mrs Romano," I say in surprise.

"Caterina," she says, her eyes filled with as much surprise as mine. "What brings you here?"

"Uh . . . is Lucian not home?" I awkwardly ask. I hope she didn't hear my words just before she opened the door. It's highly likely she did, though.

"No, you just missed him," she answers, and my mood deflates. "May I ask what this is about? I take it it's not just a friendly visit."

The way she stares at me, with those narrowed eyes, makes me uneasy. I feel like she can see right through me. But it's not like I can tell her the truth. I can't tell her I'm about to ask her son to marry me to get out of marrying a complete stranger, now can I? She would freak out.

"Well . . ." I trail off, cut off by another voice.

"Oh, Mom, I forgot something —"

He cuts himself off when he sees me.

"Because I missed him!" I exclaim, wrapping my arms around Lucian's neck. He stares down at me with furrowed eyebrows, unsure of what's happening. I lean upwards, whispering in his ear, "I'll explain later. Just help me right now.

Please."

He doesn't hesitate in wrapping an arm around my waist and pulling me flush against him. I gasp in surprise. We've been this close before, but somehow, it feels different this time. I just can't pinpoint why.

His mother stares at us with slightly widened eyes.

"You know we've always been close, right, Mom?"

He leans his head against mine, and I awkwardly laugh, instinctively tightening my arms around him. His mother mimics my laugh, waving it off.

"Of course," she says, her voice hesitant. "You two have always been good friends."

She calls us friends, but the way she eyes his arm on my waist says something else. It's almost as if she knows something I don't. It unsettles me.

"Well, I checked on you, so I'll get going now," his mother says, reaching inside the apartment to grab her bag, and then she's off without another glance at us. Weird.

"So, what brings you here?" Lucian asks, removing his arm from my waist. I try not to frown, forcing myself to let him go, as well.

"I missed you," I plainly state.

He stares at me like, *are you serious?* "Come on. Tell me the real reason," he says, walking into the apartment. And then he adds, "And why I had to help you lie to my mom back there."

I follow him inside, closing the door behind me. He produces a bottle of water from the refrigerator and twists the cap open before taking large gulps of the water. I try not to ogle the way his Adam's apple bobs with each swallow.

"I need a favour," I finally admit.

"What kind of favour?" he asks, gesturing me to follow him to the living room. He sits down on one couch, and when I want to sit on the one opposite him, he pulls me onto the couch right next to him. "I need you close for this favour."

Why would he say that when he doesn't even know what the favour is?

"So? What is it?" he asks again.

"I need you to marry me."

I didn't want to come off too strong. I wanted to ease him into this by maybe subtly giving him hints as to why marrying me would benefit him, as well. But there I went and just blurted it out, ruining everything.

He blinks. Once. Twice.

Oh no. This, his silence, can't be a good sign.

I half expect him to burst out laughing but hope that he doesn't because this is already hard for me as it is.

"Why?" he finally asks. Surprisingly, he doesn't sound angry or against the idea in his tone.

So I take that as an opportunity and proceed to tell him everything that my mother had told me. It's not much as it is, but it's enough to have me making this decision.

He listens quietly the entire time I talk, nodding every now and then. Then I'm done, and he still doesn't say anything.

"Why . . . why are you not saying anything?" I nervously ask.

"Do you want to marry me?" he asks instead of answering my question. I'm confused by his question. What does that matter? I'm asking *him* to marry *me* after all. "I need to know how you feel about this."

"I . . . it's not ideal, but you were the first person I thought of," I honestly say.

"Why? Why was I the first person you thought of? Because of what family I come from?"

I want to say no, to protest to his thoughts, but I can't.

Because he's right.

I look down shamefully.

"I'm sorry," I find myself saying. "I-I clearly didn't think this through."

I move to stand up, but Lucian just pulls me back down onto his lap this time. I yelp in surprise.

"Look, *stellina*. You know I care about you, right?" he asks. I nod. I know he does.

"I wouldn't mind marrying you, to be honest, but if you're doing this, offering this to me just because you feel that you have no other choice, I won't accept."

My eyes widen. He doesn't mind . . . marrying me?

"I-it's not like that," I protest. "I . . . yes. You came to mind first because you're a Romano. But more than that, it's because I trust you. With my life. I'd rather be with you than anyone else."

He takes in my words.

"I never dreamed about love because it never seemed possible for me, given my family situation," I confess. "But this, you . . . marrying you would be the closest thing I'd ever get to real love."

I bite my lip when I'm done speaking, watching as shock flashes in his eyes.

"What if we're not compatible?"

In bed, he means.

I shake my head. I know we are. The way my body reacts to his simplest of touches tells me this. I've never thought of sleeping with Lucian, but now that I am, I realise we are *very* compatible.

"One last question," he suddenly says, and I nod with a gulp. "Do you have any exes I need to worry about? I don't like the idea of other men still being alive after touching what's mine."

He practically growls the last part. I shake my head. There are no exes. I never had a chance to date anyone, not with my overprotective and obsessive father.

"Then my answer is yes."

I suck in a hopeful breath.
"I'll marry you."

Chapter Nine: Caterina

He said yes.

He said yes!

That's all I chant in my head as Lucian and I watch a movie on the couch. The couch where he agreed to marry me. I still can't believe he said yes. I mean, I know he'd do anything for me, but this was something else. This would tie him to me for the rest of our lives. It's not something to be taken lightly.

"What are you thinking, *stellina*?" Lucian murmurs.

I lean my head on his shoulder. "I just . . . can't believe you said yes," I admit.

"Was there ever any doubt?"

My head snaps up to his. What did he mean by that?

"There's no way I'd ever let you marry another man, *stellina*," he suddenly says, grabbing my left hand and rubbing his thumb over my ring finger. "This finger has always belonged to me, Caterina. *Always*."

My eyes widen. Is he saying what I think he's saying?

"Lucian . . ."

"Shh," he shushes me. "Watch the movie."

I try and force myself to focus on the movie, but it's hard. Especially when I can't stop thinking about what he just said merely a few moments ago. I glance down at my left hand that he holds in his. My left ring finger has always belonged to him. That's what he said.

Maybe I'm thinking too much into this, and call me naïve, but I feel like this means something.

Then he leans down and whispers in my ear, "Want to stay

over tonight?"

My breath hitches. *Do I?*

Between me asking him to marry me and him basically admitting he's always wanted to marry me, do I want to stay over?

Swallowing, I softly say, "Yes."

I feel him smile against my head.

"Can we go to bed now?" I find myself asking him, looking up at him with puppy eyes. What's happening to me? It's just like the night when he saved me at the club.

"You don't want to finish the movie?" he asks, and I shake my head. Then he grins, abruptly standing up with me in his arms, causing me to squeal. He carries me back into the hallway, stopping by the first open door and walking inside. Immediately, I know it's his room.

I can tell from the smell alone. It smells like *him*. It's like heaven for my senses.

The room is simplistic. There's a king-sized bed in the middle, covered by grey sheets along with grey pillows, and there's a window on the side of the room, with the identical grey curtains are drawn back. Then there's a door on the other side, leading to a bathroom, I'm assuming.

Lucian carries me to the bed, sitting me down gently on the edge.

"Do you want something to wear?" he asks, and I look down at myself. I'm wearing a pair of skinny jeans and a flowery top with sneakers. I nod to him, knowing that sleeping in this'll be a struggle. He disappears into the closet and emerges after a few moments, tossing me a thin grey long-sleeved shirt. I hesitate, gasping softly when he pulls his shirt over his head.

Is he expecting me to undress myself here, too?

Get a grip, Caterina. You two are getting married. You'll see each other naked.

But still. We're not married yet.

My breath hitches when he slips out of his trousers, leaving him in merely a pair of tight boxer briefs. Wow, he's *huge*. My eyes nearly pop out of their sockets with the way I stare at his bulge, and he's not even hard *yet*. I know because we haven't done anything.

He clears his throat and has me looking away immediately, coughing and pretending he didn't just catch me ogling his package.

Without thinking, I toe off my sneakers and pull the top over my head, leaving my chest bare besides a plain black bra. His breath hitches, and I realise what I've just done.

"You know what. I'll just get changed in the bathroom—"

He stops me as I make a beeline for the door. I avoid his eyes, unable to look at him. I know all my emotions will show if I do.

"*Stellina*, won't you undress for me?"

My head snaps up to his, my eyes wide. Did he just say what I think he did?

"You don't have to be shy for me," he says when I don't say anything. "We're going to be married soon anyway."

He makes a valid point.

"Should I help you?" he says, offering, but I shake my head. I need to do this myself.

I take a step away from him, popping open the button of my jeans. I shimmy out of them, stepping out and leave them lying on the floor. Now I'm standing in front of him in just my underwear, just like he is to me.

He looks a hundred times more confident than I do, but that's okay. I'm half hoping he'll lead. He steps forward, his hands landing on my bare waist.

"We'll just be sleeping tonight," he tells me, and without meaning to, I release a breath of relief. He smiles, leading me backwards towards the bed. "You can wear my shirt if that makes you more comfortable."

I bravely shake my head. Why bother hiding what he's already seen?

He smiles in satisfaction, picking me up easily and placing me under the covers. He climbs in next to me and pulls me into him, wrapping an arm around my waist. I lay my head on his bare chest, my eyes fluttering closed.

"You're really okay with this?" I can't help but ask him. He hums.

"I'm more than okay, *stellina*," he assures me, sensing my nervousness regarding the matter. "Now go to sleep."

And I do.

Falling into the deepest sleep of my life.

CHAPTER TEN: CATERINA

"This is your new phone."

Lucian hands me the latest model phone. I completely forgot that I lost my phone in the club the other night. It's funny how easily I forgot, but then again, who wouldn't when they have nobody checking up on them or friends to text.

"My number is already added. You can put whoever else's number you want in there. Your maid, for example. But no men." He says the last part as a warning, and I nod. Now that we're a thing, I'm not going after other men. Not that I ever did before.

"Thank you," I say, smiling up at him.

He reaches over the console and places his hand on the back of my head. I've noticed that he likes doing that. He rubs my head soothingly with his thumb before leaning forward and placing a soft kiss on my forehead. I can't help but frown.

Yes, he refused to kiss me before because he thought I was drunk, but what's his excuse now? If anything, now's the perfect time for us to kiss. Now that we're engaged.

We're engaged. I'm engaged to Luciano Romano. It's almost unbelievable. Except it's real. It's very real. Now, I can call someone like him my own. Lucian is *mine*.

The possessive feeling that washes over me is almost overwhelming. Is this how it feels to want someone, to have someone as your own?

"What are you thinking about, *stellina*?" Lucian asks, rubbing my head.

I smile. "Us," I easily answer. He blinks in surprise. I lean forward, bringing my face close to his. "You told me no other men. The same applies to you. No more other women."

My tone is stern, and I'm being serious. It would break my heart if I caught him with another woman like I did that day.

His eyes become serious.

"There will be no other women, *stellina*," he promises. "You're it for me."

"Also, I have a request for you," I state, and his brow raises in questioning. "The next time you think about kissing me, it won't be on my forehead. It'll be on my lips."

I've stunned him.

And then I decide it's the perfect time to hop out of the car.

I skip all the way to the house, a wide smile on my face as I walk in, but that quickly fades when I catch sight of my mother's angry eyes.

"Mama," I greet.

"Don't Mama me," she snaps. "What the hell were you just doing with Luciano Romano?"

"Nothing," I find myself lying. If we're going to tell our families we're getting married, we're doing it together. Support one another. "We're *friends*, Mom."

"Didn't seem like just that to me," Mother snaps.

"You misunderstood," I say.

"He *touched* you, Caterina," Mother emphasizes.

"You know how our relationship has always been. He's always been touching me over the years, Mom. Nothing's changed," I tell her. She hesitates because she knows I'm right. Lucian has always been a touchy person with me. Even when we were little, he would always hold my hand, hook my arm around his, and pet my head. And then, when we got older, he started rubbing the back of my head, wrapped his arm around my waist, and placed kisses on my forehead. Nothing's changed.

"I'm sorry," Mother suddenly says. "It's just . . . with all these arrangements and meetings with your potential husbands, I've become sensitive."

Meetings with my potential husbands? It's that far already? And I'm still not supposed to know. Father will probably just introduce me to the chosen one and force me to marry him.

"Look, I know you're against this whole arranged marriage thing, but it really is for the best," Mother says. And then her eyes flash. "Oh, right. You said you would find yourself a husband. Have you found anyone yet?"

The fact that she doesn't see Lucian as even a potential husband is a problem. I don't understand why she's this way, though. I mean, really. What's her issue with him? If anything, he's the most suitable husband for me.

I shake my head at her question, and she sighs in relief.

"Good. I know this will be hard, but I trust your father's judgement. He'll find you a good man," Mother assures me.

No. He'll find a powerful man, and powerful men are all the same. Cold, abusive, degrading. I found a different one. Lucian. And I was lucky. But I just nod to my mother, not wanting to upset her even further.

We'll tell her later.

"Miss Russo!" Mary comes running into my bedroom, a wide smile on her face. "You're back," she breathes out.

I smile. Someone sure is happy to see me. "Come here," I say, opening my arms to her. She hugs me tightly. "Are you okay?"

"Yes, Miss Russo," she says, pulling away. "It's all because of you, Miss Russo. You took such good care of me after I was let go."

"Of course. I have to take care of you, too," I tell her, and she nods, smiling. Then I beckon her forward, like I'm about to tell her a secret, which I am. "I'm engaged."

She pulls back with wide eyes.

"No way . . ." She trails off. "Has Mr Russo already chosen a husband for you?"

So everyone here knows. Everyone but me, the actual person who's affected by this.

"No." I shake my head. "Father hasn't chosen anyone yet."

"Then?"

"I'm marrying someone else," I declare.

"Who?" she asks.

"Luciano Romano."

She gasps so loud that I have to cover her mouth with my hand.

"I'll tell you everything if you promise to be quiet," I tell her, and she nods. Removing my hand from her mouth, I tell her everything, omitting the parts where Lucian said certain things that made my body tingle. That's private. But everything else, me proposing to him and him saying yes, I tell her.

She manages to stay quiet the entire time, but her big eyes give her away. She's completely flabbergasted.

Then she smiles, pulling me into another hug.

"I'm so relieved, Miss Russo," she admits. "I was so worried, but now I don't have to be anymore. Mr Romano will take good care of you. I know it."

I wipe away a sudden stray tear.

"I'm really, really happy for you, Miss Russo."

I close my eyes, tears falling from them. I hug her tighter.

I really needed to hear that.

Chapter Eleven: Caterina

I stare shamelessly.

I watch as he punches the punching bag. Watching as his back flexes with each punch. Watching as his muscles contract when he stretches out his limbs. I'm quite shameless, staring at Lucian with no doubt lust in my eyes after inviting myself into his home when he didn't answer the door. And now I'm here, watching him punch a punching bag in his home gym. It's quite the view, and I find desire pooling in between my legs as I watch the droplets of sweat run down his spine.

He hasn't noticed me yet, his eyebrows furrowed as he focuses on what he's doing, a pair of earbuds located securely in his ears. I'm overcome with the sudden desire to go to him, to touch him, to *smell* him. That's weird, though, considering how sweaty he is. He must stink right now, right?

I don't know how much longer I just stand there in the gym's doorway, staring at my new fiancé as he works all his frustration out on a poor punching bag. He lands one final blow, sending the punching bag flying back far, and when it comes flying back, he dodges it just in time before it smacks him right in the face.

Clapping, I make my presence known. Except, he still doesn't notice me, grabbing a water bottle and gulping down large sips of water. I frown, clapping louder, but there's still no response. No recognition that he knows I'm here. Just how loud are those earbuds playing?

Sighing, I decide to walk over to him. When I reach him, I tap on his shoulder, but then suddenly, he spins around, grabbing me and tackling me to the ground. I hit the ground with a thud, him on top of me. He's glaring at me for a single moment before realisation dawns on his face, and it softens.

"*Stellina*," he says in surprise. "What are you doing here?"

Mind you, he's still not getting off me, keeping my hands above my head and pinning them down with his own.

"I came in myself when you didn't answer the door," I say, and he frowns. "And about *this*, I tried to get your attention, but it seemed like you were blocking everything out."

Now I'm the one frowning.

"I'm sorry, baby," he apologizes. "I don't know what happened. I was distracted, and when you tapped me . . . I went into attack mode. I'm sorry."

How can I possibly be mad when he ends it off with a kiss on my forehead? Wait, I can be mad because he broke the deal we made. Well, I don't know if we actually made a deal out of it, but still. He did what I told him not to do.

"What's wrong?" he asks, eyebrows furrowing.

"My lips!" I exclaim. "I told you before."

He looks confused until it dawns on him, and his lips form an *oh*.

Oh is his only response? Oh? That's it? Does he *not* want to kiss me?

He lets go of my wrists and moves to get off me, but I lock my legs around his waist, keeping him in place, and this causes him to freeze. I cup his face in between my hands, forcing a determined look onto my face.

"Are you really going to make me do it myself?" I question, but he's frozen in my hold, blinking through his surprise.

Then, without another thought, I lift my head, leaning upwards, and place my lips on his. It's quick, just a little peck before I pull away. He looks completely stunned by what I just did, and suddenly, I'm pushing him off me, touching my lips in disbelief. Did I really just do that? Did I really just kiss him? And against his own will?

God, I'm such a terrible person. Yes, he's my fiancé, but that doesn't give me the right to forcefully kiss him.

Groaning, I rush to my feet and head straight for the door. However, I don't get far before an arm wraps around me, and I'm pulled back into a hard chest. I stay still, keeping my eyes glued to the floor even though we aren't even standing face to face.

"I'm sorry," I quickly apologize. "I didn't mean to ... I wasn't thinking."

It's a lame excuse, but it's the truth. I really wasn't thinking when I kissed him, not about him or the consequences. I just wanted to kiss him. That's all I knew and still know.

"Why are you sorry?" he asks.

"Because I forcefully kissed you when you clearly didn't want to," I mumble, shame washing over me. Why am I like this, really?

"You really think I didn't want to kiss you?" he murmurs, his lips right by my ear. I feel it all the way down to my toes.

I suck in a breath.

"I wanted to kiss you," he admits, dragging the tip of his nose all the way down to my neck. I shiver. "I wanted to kiss you so badly I thought I might combust in my sweats."

My eyes widen. He wanted to kiss me? He wanted to kiss me *that* badly?

I try to turn around in his arms, but he holds me in place.

"Let me see you," I whisper. "Please."

He shakes his head. Then suddenly, he places a kiss on the base of my neck, an involuntary gasp escaping me.

"You like that?" he asks, and I nod. "Use your words, baby."

"Y-yes," I stammer, my cheeks flushing in embarrassment. Then he spins me around abruptly, and finally, I can look at him again, and I'm surprised by what I see.

His cheeks are flushed, his eyes dark, and his pupils dilated. He's *aroused*. All by a simple peck? But then again, I became hot when all I did was watch him work out, so I guess I'm no better.

"Do you see what you do to me?" he murmurs, his voice husky. I can't help but look away and then down, my eyes widening when I see the very *obvious bulge* in his sweats. Oh, he's *really* turned on.

I look away immediately, unsure of where to look that won't turn me into a ripe tomato, but he doesn't leave me be, gripping my chin in between his fingers and turning my head so that I'm looking at him again.

When he sees how flushed I am, he smiles.

"Do I make you nervous?" he asks, and I hesitantly nod. "Use your words, baby."

He repeats the same words he used earlier.

"Y-yes," I stutter. "You make me nervous."

"Good girl," he praises. There it is, the praise kink again, making my legs feel weak.

He tilts my chin up with his fingers, and a vein in my exposed neck pulses. He doesn't miss it, his eyes flashing with something that's never been directed at me before, and so I have no idea what it means.

"Have you kissed someone before? Besides that peck just now, of course," he asks.

I gulp, nodding. "Once," I tell him the truth. "It was when I was still a teenager. I snuck out of school to go make out with a boy at his place."

His eyes darken. "And then what happened?" he questions, his grip on my chin tightening.

"And then we . . . kissed," I say, embarrassed by my confession.

"And then what? Did he fuck you?" I flinch at the harshness of his voice. He's getting angry. His grip tightens even more to the point that I think it may leave a bruise behind. "Tell me, Caterina. Did you let him fuck you?"

I shake my head. "No!" I exclaim. "One of Dad's guards burst through the door before anything could happen."

"And if he hadn't?" he challenges, and I purse my lips, uncomfortable by this whole conversation. "Would you have let that *boy* fuck you?"

"I-I don't know," I confess. The truth is, that was the day after I begged my father to go on the school trip, and he vehemently refused. I was so angry that I would've done anything to piss him off. That included losing my virginity to the school bad boy with probably a whole set of STDs. I know it was stupid, but I was young, and I'd like to think I didn't know any better, especially when no one ever taught me anything about boys and sex.

Lucian's growl startles me, and I go stumbling back a few steps in surprise. He catches me, wrapping an arm around me and pulling me back into him. When I look up at him, into his eyes, I see rage. Pure and utter *rage*.

Does the thought of me having been with another male really bother him so much?

"What about you?" I suddenly become angry, too. "Why are you getting angry at me when, just the other day, I caught you with a girl?"

His eyes flash with surprise, and then it's followed by guilt. "Because I'm a jealous fucker," he says, pulling me closer. "And I don't like the thought of another having touched or touching what's mine."

"Then what about me? Do you think I like it?" I exclaim. I hate the jealousy that wraps around me, and instead of it being a warm blanket-like feeling, it's cold and heavy and *suffocating*.

I've never felt jealous before. Not before him. And now that I'm feeling it, I hate it. I hate him.

I force myself to push him away, escaping his arms and taking a few steps away from him.

"*Stellina . . .*" He trails off.

"It's not fair," I tell him, wrapping my arms around myself. "And you know it."

"I'm sorry, baby," he says, starting off, his arms reaching out to me, but I just move away more from him. He breathes out a harsh breath. "What can I do? How can I fix this?"

"You can kill all the women you've slept with," I dare tell him.

"Done," he easily agrees, surprising me. I didn't really mean it. God, I'm so stupid. Of course if I tell him to do it, he'll do it. It's well within his capabilities. "What else?"

"You could let me fuck another man before we get married." Now I'm tip-toeing across dangerous territory. I don't actually want to do that, at least not anymore, but he doesn't know that. I know he doesn't when I see the way his entire face morphs into one of rage.

"I will not allow anything of the sort." He practically growls, his eyes daring me to protest, daring me to defy him.

Part of me wants to, just to get a reaction out of him, but for what purpose? It's no use, not when he won't allow him and not when I certainly don't want to sleep with a random man.

He grabs my arms and pulls me back to him, and this time, I let him.

"Now, if I do what you told me to, can we put this behind us? Will you forgive me?" he asks, his eyes pleading with me.

I find myself nodding, even though the thought of him possibly killing every woman he's ever been with sounds pretty crazy.

He smiles, reaching up to move a strand of hair out of my face. "Have you eaten yet?" he asks, and I shake my head with a pout. He laughs. "Let's get some food in you then."

He leads me out of the gym and to the kitchen. He starts walking to the refrigerator, but I grab his arm, stopping him.

"You reek," I bluntly say, although it's a lie. He could be sweating buckets, but he'd still smell good. I won't tell him that, though. "I'll make breakfast."

He pouts at my insult but listens nonetheless, disappearing down the hall.

Smiling, I shake my head at his impossible cuteness before going to the refrigerator and pulling it open. There's not much in there, so I grab a loaf of bread with eggs and start making French toast. I plate them nicely when I'm done, pouring just a little syrup over the slices. If there's one thing I've noticed about Lucian over the years, it's that he likes things simple, nothing too extravagant, just like me.

When he returns, he's showered and smells like his shower gel mixed in with his natural body scent. He's changed into a pair of shorts but leaves his chest bare. Typical male, I roll my eyes.

"Smells good," he says, hopping onto a bar stool. I can't help but eye his abs as he starts eating. He's sitting *and* leaning over, but not a roll in sight. How unfair is that?

I can't help but look down at myself. I have exactly two rolls when I sit down, and even though I've never minded having them before, the thought of Lucian one day seeing me naked and seeing my rolls and stretch marks makes me consider starting to work out. I mean, our families don't know about our engagement yet, so that gives me some time to slim down, right?

"What are you doing?"

My head snaps up to find Lucian frowning at me. "Nothing," I lie.

"You know I hate lies," he reminds me, but I keep quiet. "Don't make me come over there, bend you over this kitchen island and spank you."

My eyes widen, not only in shock but because of the promise in his words. He's *serious*.

"Do . . . what kind of woman do you like?" I ask, staring unsurely at him.

He frowns. "Why are you asking me that?" he questions.

"Never mind." I shrug. "Is the food okay?"

"Don't change the subject, *stellina*," he warns. "Tell me why you asked me that."

"Don't . . . don't guys like you like . . . like super skinny girls?" I can't hold in my stutter.

"What does that have to do with . . ." He trails off when he sees how I look at myself. "Oh, baby . . ."

He hops off the stool and comes to me, wrapping me in his arms. I lean my cheek against his chest, seeking the kind of comfort only he can give me.

"Are you feeling insecure?" he asks, and I nod, trying hard to hold the tears in. "Why?"

"Because I'm not . . . I don't look like those supermodels you used to date." I sniffle.

"No, you're not," he confirms, my heart plummeting to my stomach. He agrees with me. "Because you're so much better."

"What?"

He pulls away slightly so that he can look down at me.

"Most of those supermodels go on crazy diets or fast to stay so thin. Some even take steroids to lose weight. Many of them suffer from bulimia and anorexia as a result," he tells me. "But you, *stellina*. You don't do any of those things. You just live your life, and that makes you so real. This, you, your body, it's all real, and I already love it without even really seeing all of it."

He's stumped me. Completely. "How . . ." How did he know exactly what to say and so sincerely?

Because he means it, my subconscious yells at me.

He does, doesn't he? He loves my body. This gives me new-found hope. He already loves my body.

Now, I'm going to make him love *me*.

CHAPTER TWELVE: LUCIANO

I lay the pictures out in front of me.

Dante stands in front of me, eyebrows furrowed.

"What's this?" he questions.

"I need you to find these girls for me," I tell him.

"For what reason?" he asks, and I sigh.

"Can't you just do this favour for me without any questions?"

He narrows his eyes at me before he picks up one single photo, his eyes scanning it.

"All right," he says, placing it back down before piling them all on top of one another. "I'll find them for you. But what's in it for me?"

I roll my eyes. Of course. He can never do me a favour just because I'm his brother. He has to get something out of it.

"I'll find a nice girl for you," I offer.

He scoffs. "Are you fucking kidding me?" he snaps.

I smile tightly. "Okay, what do you want?" I ask him, gritting through my teeth. I may be his baby brother, but that doesn't mean very much to him.

"Tell me who these girls are," he says with a smirk. "I'm too curious, so I'll let you off the hook with this."

"Why are you so curious?" I ask him.

"Well, I assumed since you and the Russo girl were finally getting closer, you'd cut other girls out of your life," he says, and fuck it, he's right.

"These are girls I fucked before her." I force myself to tell him.

"And she wants to meet them to . . . what? Get some advice as to what you like in the bedroom?" he says, teasingly.

I glare at him. Why does everything have to be a joke with him? Oh, that's right, because he sees women as a joke. "No, she wants them dead," I bluntly say.

He blinks in surprise before he smirks. "Now that's a Russo woman for you," he says, sounding proud.

"She's *mine*," I say with a growl, feeling a possessiveness for her wrapping around me like a thick cloud.

He holds up his hands in defence. "All yours," he agrees. "I'm not into prude little virgins anyway."

I feel like punching him. I should punch him for speaking that way about *stellina*, but I hold myself back, for now. After he finds those girls for me, I'll rethink it. I'll rethink it really hard.

"So you'll find them for me?" I need confirmation from him. I need his word because, in our family, his word is pure gold.

"I did say I would," he says, picking up the stack of photos. "There's quite a lot of them, so it may take a while."

"You have one week," I tell him, my tone conveying how serious I am and that I'm not up for negotiation on that.

"I'll have them all in three days," he says instead, and I nod.

When it comes to the mafia business, I can always count on Dante.

"You know," he suddenly starts speaking again. "If you need any help torturing and killing these girls, I'd be happy to help."

Of course he would be.

"Come on," he says when I don't respond. "Let me in on the fun."

Sighing, I mutter, "Whatever."

He smiles so broadly that it's nearly blinding. Wow, I

haven't seen him smile in *years*. It's kind of really fucking scary. And him getting this excited over the prospect of torturing and killing a bunch of women screams *red flag*. Not that I care. I'm not going to be his lover anyway. So why should I care if he's a walking red flag or not?

"Since that's all, I'll be on my way now," I say, saluting him before moving to walk out of his office. He stops me, though.

"I heard something interesting," he suddenly says, his lips curling upwards into a smirk.

"And it should interest me, why?" I ask, my tone bored. Because I am bored.

"Because it has to do with your girl," he simply says.

"What about her?" I growl.

"A little birdie told me her father's looking for a suitable spouse for her," he tells me.

"A little birdie?" I narrow my eyes at him.

"Okay, so I wasn't going to tell you because we all know how you get when you're pissed off . . ." He trails off.

"Spit it out already!" I snap.

"Her father came to me with a preposition," he starts off. "A preposition of marriage."

What? Her father wants to find her a suitable spouse, and he approached *Dante*?

Dante is literally the worst kind of person he could have set his daughter up with. But why? If he wants someone from the Romano family, why not approach me? Oh, right, because Dante is the Don, and I'm merely the younger brother with nothing to his name.

"So what did you say?" I question, glaring at him. He lifts his hands up in defence.

"Hey, I declined," he assures me. "I don't want to get married and be tied down to one person for the rest of my life."

Of course. Dante enjoys the bachelor life with a different woman in his bed each night.

"But . . . just because I said no doesn't mean another man will, too," he tells me, staring pointedly at me.

"I know." I breathe out. "I know that more than you think."

Then suddenly, my phone rings, and *her* name flashes on my screen.

"Answer it. I won't eavesdrop," Dante says when he sees my hesitation before busying himself with some paperwork.

I answer the call without another thought.

"Yes, *stellina*?" I talk into the phone, worry creeping in when I hear how heavy and unsteady her breathing is. "Baby, what's wrong?"

Despite Dante saying he wouldn't eavesdrop, his eyes flicker up to me.

"Lucian," she whispers into the call, like she's afraid she'll be caught. By what, or who, though? "My father called me and my sisters to a family meeting, saying that he has an important announcement."

I growl lowly.

The two of us aren't stupid. After what he's been busy with for the last few weeks, there's only one announcement he may want to make. He found Caterina a husband.

Fuck.

"Lucian, what do I do?" she whispers.

Fuuuuuuck.

"Don't worry. I'll be there soon," I assure her, not giving her a chance to respond before hanging up. Running my hands through my hair, I take a step back towards the door. "I have to go."

Dante doesn't ask any questions, thankfully, and I'm out the door.

No way in hell am I letting another man take what's mine.

Chapter Thirteen: Caterina

I'm nervous.

My palms are sweaty and clammy. My two sisters, Alba, and Viola, our mother, our father, and I all sit in the living room. Only three of us in the room know why we're having this meeting, whereas my two sisters are in the dark.

Honestly, I'm a little upset, not at them, but because of my father's screwed-up logic. Both Viola and Alba are older than me, and so shouldn't he have arranged a marriage for one of them first? I mean, Alba barely does anything with her life outside this house. Viola has been out and about since moving out, probably tainting our family image with her promiscuous ways. So why isn't he forcing her to settle down? Why me, the youngest? If anything, I still have a good few single years of my life left.

"So," Father suddenly speaks up, clasping his hands together. "You all must be wondering why you're here."

I resist the urge to scoff, glaring at my mother. She has a guilty look in her eyes, but she stands by Father's side nonetheless. She was supposed to be on *my* side. I'm her daughter. But no matter what, no matter what Father does or how many affairs he has, she still stays there by his side, through it all. I'd never, no matter how much I love someone. But then again, this isn't about love, is it? It's more about *who* my father is and how she'd be nothing without him.

"I've decided that it's time for one of you to get married."

Alba remains silent while Viola gasps in horror. Of course she doesn't want to be tied down. But she's lucky because this isn't about her.

"Caterina," Father calls out, his eyes set on me, and this time, it's Alba who reacts, her head snapping toward me with wide eyes. "I've found a suitable husband for you."

He smiles at that like he's pleased with himself. I'm sure he is.

"You'll be marrying Adrian Ricci."

My eyes widen. Adrian Ricci? He's like, forty years old, twice my own age. He's also a very disgusting man, who's known for his paedophilic tendencies.

"Papa," Alba gasps out. "Caterina is far too young for that man."

"Her age doesn't matter," Father says. "She's of legal age and adult now, and so she can marry an older man."

But Adrian Ricci isn't just an older man. He's an *older* man.

I think back to my phone call to Lucian earlier. He said he was on his way, but that was a while ago, and he's still not here. He couldn't have changed his mind, could he? Because if he did, I'm screwed, both figuratively and literally, all by Mr Adrian Ricci.

"Caterina, darling," Father calls out, capturing my attention. "You don't object to this marriage, do you?"

There's a hopeful look on his face, but the glint in his eyes tells me something else. Dare object, and you'll see what happens. The threat is clear.

Lucian . . . where are you?

"Caterina," Father calls out again, his voice harsh. "Do you object?"

Alba stares at me worriedly while Viola busies herself with a hangnail. She never cared much about me from the very beginning. Well, more like not at all.

"I . . . I—"

The door flings open, and a familiar person bursts in. Thank God.

"Mr Romano, what are you doing here?" Mother gasps out, but he comes to me first, cupping my face in between his hands.

"Are you okay?" he asks, the concern in his eyes causing me to tear up. I sniffle, shaking my head.

Lucian stands up straight again, his eyes set on my father now.

"Luciano, we are in the middle of a family meeting. This is no time for you to show your insolence."

Lucian scoffs. "My insolence?"

Something flickers in Father's eyes at Lucian's tone. Something like fear.

"What about you? Are you not being insolent yourself by forcing your daughter to marry a man twice her age?" Lucian snaps, and everyone in the room flinches, all except me. I know him better than this, and I know that however harshly he may come off, he would never hurt *me*, and so I'm not afraid.

But wait . . . how does he know who my father wants me to marry? I don't recall ever telling him. Hell, I didn't even know until just now. So how did he . . . of course. He's Luciano Romano. He can find out anything, even with limited time.

"She's my daughter, so whoever she marries is up to me." Father tries to argue, rising to his feet. He's trying to stand tall, to intimidate Lucian, but he's a good few inches shorter than him, and he's so scrawny compared to my fiancé that it's almost embarrassing for me.

"I won't allow it. Caterina will not marry Adrian Ricci," Lucian says, spitting the words out. There's promise in those words, a promise that puts me at ease.

"And who are you to decide this?" Father challenges.

"Her fiancé," Lucian snaps out. My sisters, mother, and father all gasp. I rise to my feet, grabbing onto Lucian's hand.

He squeezes mine, sending me an assuring nod.

"This is crazy," Father mutters. "How can you two be engaged?"

"I chose him," I finally speak up. "I picked him to be my husband, and you will respect that."

Father stares at me in disbelief. Mother looks like she wants to cry. The only person who looks genuinely happy and relieved for me is Alba, as to be expected.

"That's right," Lucian says, turning to look at me with such sincerity in his eyes that my heart clenches in the most amazing way in my chest. "We will be married soon, and there's nothing you can do to try to stop us."

And then he kisses me.

I gasp into his mouth. This kiss . . . it's nothing like the peck I gave him back at his home gym. No, this is more intense, more hungry, just *more.*

I'm hesitant at first, my hands lame at my sides. And then suddenly, something in me snaps, and I'm wrapping my arms around his neck, pulling him closer. He grabs a fistful of my hair, and I can't help the moan that tumbles from my lips.

This kiss . . . it's incredible. Is this what I've been missing out on all these years? My little make-out session from high school was nothing compared to this. This is so much more and makes me feel so much more. If I could, I'd keep his lips glued to mine. I'd never stop kissing him. Ever.

But unfortunately, I need to breathe, and I'm forced to break away from him, sucking in the breath that he stole when he kissed me so abruptly.

His breaths come out unsteady but not nearly as erratic as mine.

"What the fuck!"

I flinch back to reality, instinctively pressing myself deeper into Lucian's hold upon seeing the rage in my father's eyes. He wraps his arms around my shoulders, keeping me to him, thankfully, and glares at my father. His glare is so fierce that my father cowers, surprising all of us. Where did the father we all know go? Why is he submitting?

"I trust you have no objections?" Lucian speaks, his eyes on my father. Father nods, beads of sweat visibly forming on his forehead. Then Lucian's eyes are back on me. "Good. Now, *stellina*, why don't you show me your bedroom?"

The mischievous glint in his eyes is one he doesn't bother, or rather, care to hide.

But I find myself nodding, grabbing his hand and leading him up to my bedroom, ignoring everyone's dropped jaws. When we stop in front of my bedroom door, I hesitate. My bedroom is *very* girly and pink and not much has been changed since I was a little girl. I even still have that collection of stuffed bears in all different colours and sizes. It didn't bother me before, but now that I'm about to show it to Lucian, I can't help but feel like it's probably too childish for his liking.

But before I can tell him we should just go back downstairs, he's opening the door and walking inside.

"Lucian!" I exclaim. He chuckles when he sees my bedroom, and I lower my head in embarrassment. Luckily, there are no boy band posters plastered all over the walls. I was always a princess girl, no matter what age I was.

I try to cover his eyes with my hands, but he's just too damn tall.

"Don't look," I whine.

"Why?"

"It's embarrassing," I admit, looking down.

"*Stellina*," he calls out softly, lifting my chin with his fingers. "There's nothing to be embarrassed about, certainly not about the things you like."

"But I am," I tell him with a pout. Then he does the most unexpected thing. He kisses it away.

My eyes widen, and my cheeks warm up. Did he just kiss me . . . again?

"You don't have to be, baby. I love everything about you, including what you find embarrassing," he assures me.

"Really?"

He nods. I smile.

"Now, the question is, would you find it weird that I want to make out with you on your princess-themed bed in a bedroom full of stuffed bears?"

I burst out laughing, shaking my head and pulling him into a hug.

"Thank you," I say.

"For what?" he asks, resting his chin on the top of my head.

"Everything."

Chapter Fourteen: Luciano

Three days.

That's how long he said it would take. And it was exactly three days before Dante calls me. I join him in our headquarters in the basement, where we torture our enemies. He's already got them all ready for me when I arrive, all buck naked and tied to the ceiling with chains.

Dante's face has a sick smile as he stares at them, like he wants to devour them. But they're untouched besides a few cuts and bruises from capturing them, probably.

"I'm surprised the floor isn't dripping with blood yet," I muse, staring pointedly at my brother.

He shrugs. "This is for *your* girl, after all," he says. "You should show her it was you who did this to them."

He's quite caring . . . in his own sick and twisted way.

I look at the girls, their faces barely familiar to me. That just proves how unmemorable they were. That, and because I only had one person on my mind the entire time.

"Lucian—" one woman says.

I slap her across the face before I even realise it. Only my *stellina* can call me Lucian. No one else.

She coughs out blood, staining her lips red with it.

I see the wicked look on my brother's face in my peripheral.

"Can I start now?" he asks, and I nod. I honestly don't care if he's the one who ends up killing them all. As long as they're dead by the end of this.

Dante walks over to a table that has a variety of different

sharp weapons on it, trailing his fingers over each of them teasingly, adding to the horror of our victims. Then he makes his first choice, a hammer. He doesn't say a word, silently walking to the back of the room, finding his first victim. Then he jams the hammer into her skull, her screams echoing throughout the place. I know that one hit was enough to kill her, but Dante just continues, blood splattering all over his clothes and face.

The man is a fucking psycho.

Then he moves on to the next victim, grabbing a knife. He drags it all the way down her face, no doubt scarring her before plunging the knife into her throat. Blood goes everywhere, and the sick bastard laughs. He fucking *laughs*.

He kills three more girls before handing me the knife. I end the rest of their lives easily, with one stab to their vital points.

"You're so boring," Dante whines from beside me.

Dropping the knife to the floor, I wipe my bloody hands with a white cloth.

Dante instructs the man standing guard watching the entire thing to take pictures and have them delivered to me.

"Well, that was fun," he says, a twisted look on his face. He looks satiated, like a man who's just had the best fuck of his life. I bet he finds more thrill in killing people than being buried inside a woman.

"Thanks," I say to Dante, who nods, saluting me.

Then I leave.

I pull up in front of the Romano household.

When I walk in, I head straight to my father's office, knowing that the news of my engagement has probably already reached his ears, and he'd definitely want to see me about it.

I knock on the door, hearing a soft come in before opening the door and walking in.

"I was hoping you'd come see me," Father says before I can

even greet him. He gestures to the chair on the opposite side of his desk. "Sit down."

I sink into the seat.

"So I heard something very interesting," he starts off with, staring at me through blank eyes. "Your engagement to Caterina Russo, is it the truth?"

"Yes," I say with a nod. "We're going to get married."

Father smiles with a shake of his head.

"I always knew you had a thing for her since you were younger, but a part of me always thought it was just a phase and that you'd get over her at some point," he admits. "Never did I think you'd actually want to marry this girl."

I try not to feel offended. My feelings for *stellina* were never a phase. It was real, as real as anything can be.

"Do you object to this marriage?" I ask.

Father shakes his head. "Not at all. In fact, after what Alessandro did, I'm more than pleased with your choice of a wife."

I purse my lips at the mention of my older brother. Just like I'm about to do, Alessandro married for love. Unfortunately, his choice just wasn't worthy enough in Father's eyes.

Speaking of Alessandro, I should invite him to my wedding. Father will most definitely protest, especially if Havyn is his date, but I don't care. He's my brother, and I want him there.

"Although, I do have one concern," Father suddenly says. I narrow my eyes at him. "I also heard that she was actually supposed to marry Adrian Ricci."

"You don't have to worry about that. I took care of it," I tell him.

"Are you certain? I wouldn't want to make an enemy of the Ricci's," Father says.

I can't roll my eyes any louder. Of course.

"If there's any problems, Dante will deal with it."

The Ricci's power isn't nearly close to ours, and so they're nothing to worry about. Besides, they wouldn't dare try anything. Father is just nitpicking, being his own selfish self.

I know what this is really about. Father is selfish, and so despite me being his son, he doesn't wish me any happiness of my own. Just because he never had any happiness of his own. I won't let him get to me, though.

"Then I guess all is good," Father says, clasping his hands together.

I nod. "I'm glad," I say, eyeing him.

He better not try anything. Otherwise, I won't be held accountable for what I do.

CHAPTER FIFTEEN: CATERINA

"So, you're really marrying Luciano Romano?"

I was surprised when Viola came knocking on my bedroom door wanting to talk, because we don't talk. We just walk past one another without any acknowledgement and ignore one another's existence for the most part. But of course. I should've expected this. The only time she *really* wants to talk to me is because I'm marrying a Romano, something she's dreamed her whole life of doing.

I nod at her question, and she scoffs.

"Why you?" she questions. "What makes you so special?"

"Lucian is too young for you, Viola." I point out, although I know she's not talking about him. She's talking about *Dante*.

For as long as I can remember, Viola has been completely infatuated with Dante Romano, despite his . . . *colourful* reputation and past. None of that ever bothered her. She wanted him, and she still wants him even to this day. Too bad he's never even spared her a single glance, and that's why she acted out. Because he doesn't notice her. She might as well be invisible to him, and she hates it. That's why she goes after men lower than her because they give her the attention Dante probably never will.

Maybe if she was nicer . . .

Viola's scoff breaks me out of my thoughts. "It's not fair," she snaps. "I'm the eldest daughter. I should be the first to marry, not *you*."

The way she says that last word, referring to me, she sounds disgusted. By me.

"Then maybe you should stop sleeping around so that men will actually see you as a potential wife instead of just another hole," I blurt out, my eyes widening after the words are already out. I've never spoken to her like that before. Even if she was mean to me or belittled me, I always remained calm, took it all, and kept my mouth shut.

"What did you just say?" Her tone is low and dark. "Oh, you think because you're marrying a Romano, you can now say whatever you want to me?"

"It's-it's not like that," I say, shaking my head, but she just scoffs.

"You're a real bitch, you know that?"

I flinch at her words. No, I'm not. "I'm sorry," I find myself apologizing despite having done nothing wrong.

"If you're really sorry, call off the engagement."

My head snaps up to hers. What? "You do realise that if I don't marry Lucian, I'll be forced to marry another man twice my age, right?"

When she nods, I want to throw up.

She doesn't care about me. She never has. So why should I call off *my* engagement to please *her*? When she'd never do the same for me?

I shake my head. "I won't," I tell her, my voice determined.

"Then you're not sorry," she says, disbelief lacing her voice.

I don't care, though. Not anymore. "I guess you're right."

Her eyes widen at my words. "You bitch," she curses. "You think you're so great? Well, guess what? Without *Lucian*, you're nothing. Damn, I bet he's only marrying you because he pities you."

Now that hits me straight in the gut.

When she sees I'm on the verge of tears, she smiles. "Aw, you didn't think he actually has feelings for you, did you?"

The way she says it, she's mocking me. But I can't help but

think. Is that really true?

"Think about it, Cat," she continues. "Why would a man like Luciano Romano, who can get any *woman* he wants, willingly marry a *girl* like you?"

"Get out."

"Excuse me?"

"I said get out!" I scream.

When she doesn't move, I grab her and practically shove her out the door, slamming it closed behind her. Sliding my body down the door, I sink into my knees, the first sniffle escaping me.

Why would she say all that? Why would she hurt me like this?

On cue, my phone rings, Lucian's name flashing on the screen.

For a moment, I hesitate. I don't want him to hear me crying. It'll only make everything worse because it'll prove to him just how much of a *girl* I really still am.

But if I don't answer, he'll worry.

Wiping away my tears and clearing my throat, I answer the call.

"*Hey, baby,*" he greets.

"Hi." I try my best to sound normal.

"*I miss you.*"

Do you really? *No, Cat. Don't think like that. Viola was just trying to get into your head. Do not take this out on Lucian.*

"*Are you okay?*" Lucian asks, startling me.

"Why?"

"*It's just . . . you don't sound like yourself.*"

He noticed. Of course he did.

"*Did something happen?*"

"No, everything's okay. I'm okay," I tell him, hoping he doesn't sense that it's a lie.

"*Well then, can I still come see you?*" he asks.

"Right now's not a really good time," I say, and it's really not. At least not while I'm still trying not to cry into the call.

"*Oh*," he says, and I wince at the clear disappointment in his voice. "*Then when's a good time?*"

"I . . . I don't know." I mumble. He sighs into the call.

"*All right then. Just . . . let me know.*"

And then he hangs up.

And then the waterworks come.

God, why am I so damn weak? Why do I let Viola's words get to me so much, to the point that I practically rejected Lucian?

I didn't even tell him I missed him, too, when I did. I missed him so much.

Burying my head on my knees, I cry.

I don't know how much time I spend just sitting there, until finally, I'm all dried out.

When I stand up, I'm determined. I won't let Viola get to me. Not anymore.

Determined, I shove some clothes and undies into a duffel bag and leave the house without telling anyone.

And I head straight to Lucian's home.

Chapter Sixteen: Caterina

When I arrive at Lucian's apartment, he's not there.

So I invite myself in like I did days ago, taking a seat on the couch as I wait for him to come home. Where is he, though? He wanted to come to me, so he should have been home. Where did he go if not to me?

Then an envelope sitting on the coffee table catches my eye. Well, it's more what's written on top of it that captures my attention.

For your girl.

For your girl? Lucian's girl?

Curiosity gets the better of me, and before I even know it, the envelope is in my hands, and I'm peeling it open. I peek inside and see a stack of photos. I can't see of what, though. Maybe I should just leave it? I bet Lucian won't be happy about me snooping in on his personal stuff. But then again, we're engaged to be married, so what's his is technically mine, too, right? And I can't have him hiding things from me, especially whoever his girl is.

If it's not me, I'm going to be pissed.

So, without another thought, I tip the envelope over, and the photos come spilling out of it onto the table.

When my eyes land on the first photo, a gasp of horror escapes my lips.

It's a photo of a girl . . . but she's hardly recognizable. Her whole head is bashed in, covered and dripping with blood. The other photos aren't any better, one of the girls having their throat plunged into with a knife, I'm assuming, and blood seeping out of it and so deep that I can practically see her veins. The rest of the pictures seem . . . better, with just stab wounds to the heart or a slit to the throat.

But . . . what is all this, and why does Lucian have this?

And then it comes to me. For your girl. Me. I asked him to kill all the women he's slept with. And . . . he did it.

This is sick and twisted, but it also awakens something inside of me. Something primal. Something twists inside of me. Something dark.

I should be angry at Lucian, but he did this . . . for me.

There's a sick clench of pleasure in my chest.

Then the front door opens, and I'm scrambling to put all the photos back into the envelope, but I'm not fast enough because while I'm still busy, he's already by my side, and I freeze. When I look up at him, he isn't staring back at me. He's staring at the photos in my hand, his forehead creased with a frown.

I drop the rest of the photos onto the table, taking a step back from him. Is he mad? He can't be. This is for me in any case, so I have a right to see them, don't I?

"Are you angry?"

My head snaps up to his, my eyes wide. Is he really asking me if I'm angry at him? I thought it would be the other way around. So I shake my head.

"Then are you disgusted?"

I should be. I really should be, but . . . I'm not. If anything, I'm thankful that he would go this far for me. Just because I asked, even though I wasn't even serious. I shake my head again.

"Then? What are you feeling?" he asks, his voice trembling slightly, like he's afraid I'll reject him after this. If only he knew . . . this made me want to *never* leave him.

I lean up, wrapping my arms around his neck. "I'm thankful."

Surprise flashes in his eyes. "You're . . . thankful?" His tone is full of disbelief.

I nod, smiling up at him. "You did this because I asked, didn't you?" I ask, and he nods. "Then it's all good."

"How . . ."

"Lucian, I knew what I was getting into when I asked you to marry me. You're from the Italian mafia family, and of course, your hands aren't clean. I probably can't even begin to comprehend the things you've seen, been through, and even done. But that's okay. Because I accept it all. I'm marrying you for you, and taking all the baggage that comes along with it."

"*Stellina* . . ."

I smile, reaching up to caress his face.

And then he's leaning down and kissing me.

I immediately wrap my arms around him, pulling him impossibly closer. This is our third kiss ever, the second real one, and the first we've shared all alone. How is it possible that it just keeps getting better and better?

He pushes me back until the back of my knees hit the arm of the couch, and I fall back with a surprised squeal. I giggle, smiling up at him as he crawls over me, a mischievous glint so like him in his eyes.

I reach up and kiss him again. I can't get enough of him, the way his lips feel against mine, the taste of him on my tongue. He moans when I delve my fingers into those thick tresses and pull. His hair is so thick and strong. I pull harder. His tongue traces the seam of my bottom lip, and I part them, letting him in for the first time ever.

I moan when his tongue touches mine, and the taste of him floods my mouth. I playfully nip at the tip of his tongue with my teeth, and he copies me, just harder to the point that I gasp.

Then a thought enters my mind. Why are we kissing? The

last time, it was for show, wasn't it? But there's no one but the two of us here right now, so why are we kissing?

He immediately notices how still I've become and pulls back, staring down at me with a look I don't understand. "What's wrong?" he asks, his voice soft and gentle.

"Why are we doing this?" I ask him. "Why are we kissing?"

"Because . . . because we want to," he answers, the confusion evident in his voice and on his face.

"Exactly. Why? Why do we want to?" I question. I feel confused. A couple of weeks ago, I wouldn't even let him touch me more than a simple arm around me or a hand on my head, but now . . . now I'm kissing him. Full on. And I . . . liked it. I liked it a lot, to the point that I didn't want to stop.

"You . . ." he mutters in disbelief. And then suddenly, he's off me, gathering the photos on the table and sliding them back into the envelope.

"Lucian—"

"Don't," he cuts in. "Just don't."

He's gone down the hall before I can even respond. With a frustrated breath, I run my fingers through my hair.

What did I just do?

Chapter Seventeen: Luciano

I'm an idiot.

A fucking stupid idiot.

How could I have been so fucking stupid?

Oh, that's right. Because of the way she looked at me. Because of the way she touched my face. She said she was thankful, and I took it the wrong way.

She doesn't feel for me the way I feel for her. That much is obvious now.

Running my fingers through my hair in frustration, I step into the running shower.

I need to wash this off. This humiliation. These feelings. This fucking arousal.

I stand under the running water, leaning my forehead against the tiled shower wall with closed eyes. My mind is a traitorous fucker, flashing the memories of a few minutes ago in front of my eyes.

How her skin felt under my touch. The feeling of her lips. The taste of her tongue.

I crave it again.

Fuck, I think I'm addicted already, and that's bad.

Wrapping my fingers around my length, I find myself to have softened already. Of course, that fucking blatant rejection ruined the entire moment.

Then I hear a knock on the bathroom door. I ignore it.

I reach for the loofah, scrubbing my body harshly with it and soap. I'm not even sure what I'm doing, but I need to scrub this all off me. The feeling of her, her tongue. I need to scrub it all off.

There isn't another knock, so I assume she left. Good. I can't see her face right now. That innocent face of hers will cause me to crumble.

When I'm done, I turn off the shower and wrap a towel around my waist before leaving the bathroom. When I see *her* sitting on my bed, I freeze. No, she can't be here. I need her to fuck off. Right now.

No, you don't, my subconscious says to me. You need her here.

I ignore her, walking to my closet. I drop my towel without care for her and whether seeing me naked would make her uncomfortable and reach for a matching tracksuit.

"I'm sorry." Her voice filters in.

"Fuck off."

My words are harsh. My tone is harsh. I can practically hear her flinch.

I've never spoken to her like that before. I never felt the need to. I never *wanted* to. But now, the words leave me without control.

"You don't mean that," she says, and I can hear the sob that's lodged in her throat. Fuck, I hurt her.

I don't say anything, though. In the past, I would have rushed over to her to make her feel better. But not this time. Because her rejection fucking hurt. This time, *she* hurt *me*.

"You should leave," I say, stepping out of the closet, fully clothed. I don't dare look at her, though, because I know. If I see a trace of a tear, I'll falter.

"I'm not going anywhere," she says, standing up and approaching me. "Not before we talk."

"Talk about what?!" I burst out, turning to her. "How you fucking rejected me?"

She flinches.

"I didn't reject you," she protests. I scoff. "I'm just

confused."

"So I'm just supposed to accept that? Like I do with everything when it comes to you?" I scoff in disbelief. "Are you seriously that oblivious to what's happening here?"

Her eyes flutter up to mine. And fuck. The unspoken tears. It makes my heart clench painfully in my chest. I hate hurting her.

"Lucian . . ."

"I fucking like you, Caterina!" I yell out without control. Her eyes widen. "Do you know how hard it is, having feelings for someone who can't even care about you enough to realise that?"

"I care about you," she protests.

"Not enough." Fuck, the truth hurts.

She doesn't protest this time. She can't because she knows I'm right.

"You should leave," I tell her, turning away from her once more.

And this time, she listens.

I down my fourth beer.

Usually, I wouldn't drink this much, but fuck it. I'm going through something right now.

I need to forget. That's why I came here, to this bar, to drown my sorrows. It's pathetic, I know. This is fucking teenage behaviour, but I can't give a fuck tonight. Tonight, I just want to lose myself in alcohol.

And when a perfectly manicured feminine hand wraps around my bicep, I see another escape. I shouldn't. I really shouldn't. I'm engaged, for fucking sake.

But instead of thinking about that, I turn to the woman who sat down next to me. She's my usual type, bleach blonde hair, fake tits, fake ass. It would be so easy to take her to a hotel room right now and fuck all this hurt away.

"You here alone?" she purrs, pulling me out of my thoughts. When she parts her thighs slightly, flashing me her bright pink underwear, I think fuck it. Who even cares right now?

I nod to her questions, and she smiles. "You looking to have a good time?" she asks, fluttering her fake lashes at me.

"Always," I tell her.

She grins, leaning forward. She brushes her hand along my pants, over my crotch. "Then how about we get out of here and go somewhere more private, where I can show you a good time?" she murmurs, palming me through my pants.

She's not a hooker, I can tell immediately. She's just genuinely looking for a good time, perhaps a distraction just like me. *Perfect*.

So I down the rest of my fifth beer and pull her out of the bar with me. I drag her to the empty alleyway with me, shoving her against the wall and unbuckling my pants. I can't wait until we get somewhere private. I need this. Now.

She seems just as eager as me, pulling up her dress and parting her panties for me to slide in. I take myself out of my boxers, but when I feel it, I frown. I'm not hard at all. No, I'm fucking *soft*.

"What are you waiting for?" she whines.

To get fucking hard. To feel some sort of arousal.

But nothing. I've got nothing. I might as well be a middle-aged man in his fifties with an erectile dysfunction.

I tuck myself back into my pants and zip myself up. "Sorry, not tonight, honey," I tell the girl, walking away but not before seeing her face fall.

Cursing under my breath, I head to my car.

Why the fuck couldn't I get hard? Before, it was easy. All I needed was a willing participant, and I could do it. A one-night stand. But tonight . . . literally *nothing* happened. I couldn't get hard. Even though that girl was practically soaked and dripping for me, I couldn't do a thing. I couldn't *feel* a thing.

Stellina's face flashes in my mind.

This is all her fault. Because now that I've touched her, *tasted* her, I can't be with any other woman. This afternoon at my apartment, when my lips touched hers, I was hard like a fucking rock.

The realization hits me.

I'm in love with her. I don't just like her anymore.

I'm fucking *in love* with her.

Fuck.

CHAPTER EIGHTEEN: CATERINA

I miss him.

I never thought I'd ever feel this, this longing to see someone, never mind Luciano Romano.

But I do. I miss him so much. He hurt me that day. He told me to literally fuck off. He's never spoken to me like that before. But I guess I can't blame him. Because I, too, hurt him. Maybe even more than he hurt me.

I want to fix things. I need to fix things. But I have no idea how.

"I fucking like you, Caterina! Do you know how hard it is, having feelings for someone who can't even care about you enough to realise that?"

I do care about him. I know I do. But do I care about him in *that* sense, in a romantic sense?

Of course you do, you idiot, my subconscious yells at me. Would you have kissed him and enjoyed it *that* much if you didn't even have a sliver of romantic feelings for him?

My subconscious is right. I know it is. So why in the world could I not say those words to Lucian? Why did I just leave when he told me to?

I need to go to him. Now.

But just as I open my bedroom door, Father is standing on the other side of it.

"Papa," I say in surprise.

"Can we talk?" he asks. This is the first time he's ever asked for something instead of just demanding it. I nod, following him to his office downstairs. We sit down opposite one another on the couch, and suddenly, being alone with him here makes me nervous.

I hope he's not going to go off at me like he did the day he found out about my and Lucian's engagement.

"I'd like to talk about your engagement," Father starts off. I nod my head. "Are you satisfied?"

"Excuse me?"

"Are you satisfied?" he repeats. "You said you chose Luciano."

"Yes, that's right. I did choose him," I say.

"And are you satisfied?" he asks again.

I nod once more. "I am satisfied," I tell my father.

"Do you like him?" Father suddenly asks.

I stay silent for a single moment, before I finally nod.

"Are you sure?"

"Yes, I'm sure," I say. "I like him. I like Lucian."

"Then I have no objections," he finally says, and I take a breath in relief. "I admit, I did want you to marry Adrian Ricci because of how good things would bode with an alliance with that family, but I guess the Romanos are okay, too."

"They're better," I cut in, and my father's eyes flash with surprise. "They're much better."

Father chuckles, shaking his head. "Yes, they're a very powerful family," he agrees. "*And* you're marrying for love. Something I could have never dreamt for."

I look down at my hands. It's no secret that my parents aren't exactly *in love*. It's more like they tolerate one another. Just that.

"Was there . . . was there ever someone you wanted to marry? Out of love?" I can't help but ask. Father shakes his head.

"I was engaged to your mother from the moment I was born. There was no time for me to even look at another woman," he admits.

My heart hurts for him. "But if you had the chance . . . would you go back and change things?"

Another *no*. "Yes, this is not ideal, but she gave me three beautiful daughters. I'll admit, I haven't always been the best father in terms of being loving and caring, but everything I've done, every choice I've made, was what I thought was best for you. Including you marrying Adrian Ricci."

I believe Father. As much of a bad father as he's been over the years, he's still only done what was best for us, even if it wasn't ethical. Hell, in our world, what even is ethics?

"Papa —"

Suddenly, the door bursts open, and Viola comes stomping in, her face red with anger. I resist the urge to groan. What did I do to her now?

But when I look at her, I realise. She's not looking at me. That anger isn't directed at me. It's directed at Father.

I'm confused. Out of all three of us, the daughters, she has the best relationship with our father. He always gave her the most freedom and treated her the best. There was never anything she wished for that she didn't get. So why in the world is she so angry at him?

"Tell me it's a lie," she whispers, her eyes flickering to me briefly.

Okay, this definitely has something to do with me, too.

"Tell me you did not approach Dante Romano with a marriage proposal!"

Father approached Dante with a marriage proposal? But . . . why is she so angry? She's in love with him, so shouldn't she be happy? But instead, she's yelling.

There's something I'm missing here.

"Viola, calm down." I try to calm her down with my gentle voice, but her fierce glare has me backing off.

"Don't you dare tell me to calm down," she snaps. "You couldn't be satisfied with one brother, so you just had to go after the other one, too? Whilst knowing how I feel about him?"

"What are you talking about?" I question. "Father, what's she talking about?"

Father looks down.

"Answer me!" I snap.

"It's true. I approached Dante Romano with a marriage proposal," Father finally admits. "A proposal to marry *you*, Caterina."

I'm stunned. Father wanted me to marry . . . Dante?

"Why?" I whisper.

"Because I initially wanted you to marry into that family, but you chose the wrong brother. I wanted you to marry the Don, not the reckless younger brother."

Viola sobs from beside me. I look up at her. Now she just looks sad, tears streaming down her pretty face. The heartbreak on her face has me wanting to hug her and tell her everything will be okay, but I know she won't let me. So I refrain.

"But he rejected it?" I ask to clarify.

Father nods.

I turn back to Viola. "Viola, I think it's time you tell Dante how you feel."

"Are you insane?"

"No, I'm not. This will keep on happening if you don't do something. Next time, it won't be me but someone else. So you need to act now. Tell him how you feel."

She stares at me through tear-soaked lashes. I nod in encouragement. I know Dante isn't the best man and that he has a really questionable reputation, but if she feels this strongly about him, I won't stop her.

"I love him," she admits to me for the first time.

I breathe out in relief. "Okay. Then let's go tell him that," I say with a nod.

"Together?" she asks. I've never seen Viola look so

vulnerable before, and despite everything she's done to me and put me through, I nod.

If she needs me, I'll be there.

Chapter Nineteen: Caterina

Coming to Dante's office alone might've been a mistake. I realise this as I stare at the armed guards surrounding the entire building. I wanted to call Lucian, but after how things ended between the two of us the last time we spoke, I hesitated, and eventually, I decided that we'd do this alone. Viola and me.

"Miss Russo," a guard greets. "How can I help you?"

"Is Mr Romano inside?" I ask, and he nods. "I have something very important to tell him. Please let him know that I'm here."

He nods again and moves away from us to talk into the walky-talky. Several minutes later, he lets us in. He leads us straight to Dante's office, not letting our eyes linger on the rest of the building for too long.

When we reach a door on the top floor that has a sign with Dante's name on it, the guard knocks once before walking away.

"Come in," I hear from inside the office.

"It's okay," I say, offering Viola a reassuring smile. "It'll all be okay. I'm here."

She nods, and then I push open the door and walk inside with Viola in tow. Dante looks surprised to see me, but barely acknowledges Viola.

"Caterina, what brings you . . . and your sister here?" he questions in surprise. It makes me think. Does he even know her name?

"*Viola* here has something to tell you," I announce.

His eyebrows furrow in confusion, but he nods, gesturing to Viola to start.

When she hesitates, I give her hand a little squeeze in encouragement.

"Do you know my name?" she asks.

"Viola Russo," he answers easily.

She nods. "Then what else do you know about me?" she asks.

"Nothing but your name," Dante admits.

She flinches at the bluntness of it. "Would you be interested in getting to know me better?"

Dante narrows his eyes at her. "Getting to know you *how*?" he questions, needing clarification.

She gulps under his intense gaze. "Romantically," she finally says.

"Romantically?" he repeats. She nods. "I'm not interested."

"What?" she blurts out.

"I'm not interested in getting to know you or any other woman romantically," he tells her, straightforward with his words. He doesn't even look slightly empathic when her lips tremble as she tries to hold in her tears. "Now, if you'll excuse me. I have important work to tend to."

"I'll be good to you!" she suddenly exclaims.

"That's not what this is about," he says.

She shakes her head. "I heard the story. Of the woman you fell in love with."

His eyes darken.

"She broke your heart, but I won't do that."

"Enough," he says, his voice deadly calm. "Don't you dare speak a word about her."

"She hurt you —"

"I said enough!" he bursts out, slamming his fist onto the desk. Now he's finally lost it. His cool. "You talk about her one more time, and I'll cut out your tongue so that you may never speak again." He's warning her, but there's promise in his words.

"Viola," I say, grabbing onto her arm. "Let's go."

She lets me pull her out of the office, the waterworks breaking out once we're outside and alone.

"How could he talk to me like that? How could he say that to me?"

Her voice is filled with disbelief at what just happened.

"I'm sorry," is all I can say.

"He still loves her," she mutters. "Whoever that bitch of a woman is. He still loves her."

I don't say anything because I know that it's useless to try and protest with her. Because I know that it's true.

Then suddenly, she's wiping away the tears that have fallen and glares up at the building.

"I need a distraction," she announces and then starts walking away from me.

"Where are you going?" I call out, following her.

"To a place where I can fuck my problems away."

A one-night stand. She's off to have a one-night stand with a random stranger.

Then suddenly, she stops and turns to me, like a light bulb just went on in her head. "Or you know what. I won't fuck a stranger. I'll just get Luciano to do it."

"What?"

"What better way to get back at Dante than fucking his brother?" she chuckles. "And I bet he'd enjoy it."

"He's my fiancé, Viola!" I yell out. I can't believe she just said that. I know she's not a good person, but I never thought she would ever stoop this low.

"So what?" she exclaims, throwing her arms up in the air. "Come on, baby sister. Your big sister is hurting. Can't you make this little sacrifice for her?"

She's trying to guilt-trip me. To get me to empathize with

her. But it won't work. Not when it comes to Lucian.

"He's *mine*," I growl.

Her eyes widen in surprise.

"You'll die by my hands before you lay a single finger on him."

And that's a promise.

Chapter Twenty: Luciano

There's a knock on the door.

I leave the couch where I was lounging to open it. I barely have time to see who it is before a body launches itself at me, and a pair of lips are attached to mine.

The moment I taste *her*, I stop resisting. It's *stellina*.

I kiss her back, delving my hands into her hair. She pushes me back into the apartment, kicking the door closed behind her. The way she's kissing me . . . it's frantic, and the way she's gripping my shirt . . . it's like she wants it off.

Breaking the kiss, I grip her arms to hold her in place when she tries to kiss me again.

"Baby, what's going on?" I breathe out.

"I want you. Is that good enough?" she answers, reaching out to unbutton my shirt.

"No," I force myself to say, even though I've hardened to a rock already. "Why do you want me? Can you promise me you won't hurt me again?" I sound pathetic, but I have to be sure. I won't let this woman hurt me like that again. I won't let her reject me again.

She pauses, looking up at me through fluttery lashes.

"How about I show you?" she murmurs, her free hand grazing over my crotch.

That's my undoing, and I'm lifting her off the ground into my arms. Her legs automatically come to wrap around my waist, squeezing me as I carry her to my bedroom.

When I get to my room, I drop her back down onto her feet and climb onto the bed, resting my back against the headboard.

"Now you can show me," I tell her, staring pointedly at her. Knowing Caterina and our very complicated relationship, I expect her to turn around and leave, coming to the conclusion that this is a mistake, that *I* am a mistake, but surprisingly, she doesn't. Instead, she approaches me very slowly, like a predator watching over their prey before pouncing.

It makes me twitch in my pants in anticipation.

I'm not exactly sure what to expect. Yes, she told me that she made out with some boy in high school and that they didn't fuck, but that doesn't mean they didn't do *other* things, and although the thought of the two of them together and him giving her a few of her firsts makes me want to rip his balls from his body, I'm curious. What has she come to learn over the years? What is she about to do to me?

She crawls over me onto the bed, straddling my thighs. She continues unbuttoning my shirt before leaving it open. She gasps when she sees my bare chest. It's not the first time she's seen me shirtless, but she's looking at me like it is. Fuck, there's something very attractive about the look in her eyes, the innocence clouding her irises. If she's gasping from just seeing my chest bare, I can't even imagine how it'll be when she sees my cock for the first time.

I can't wait.

She trails her fingers across and then down my chest, dragging her nails down each ab, like she's counting them, one by one.

I have to hold in my groan. She's going so slow, it's fucking torture. I want to touch her so badly, but I refrain. I'm not the one that has to prove myself here. I've done that plenty of times, even if she didn't realise it. Now, it's her turn.

She smiles up at me when her fingers reach my sweats, tugging at the strings playfully.

"Off?" she asks, the faux innocence she puts into her voice

making me twitch in those very sweats. I lift my hips, giving her a silent answer and letting her pull them down my legs. My cock springs free since I went commando today, so hard that it stands up against my abs.

Stellina gasps when she sees it — my cock — for the first time. "You're . . . so big."

Fucking hell. I nearly bust a nut at those words.

She sounds so fucking fascinated by my cock, her eyes wide and unmoving from it. When she touches it, just a simple tap, it twitches, and she jumps back, startled. She looks up at me for . . . something, I have no idea what, but I nod.

Then she wraps her hand around the base of me, the pre-cum already leaking out from the head, which she surprises me by leaning down and licking off.

This time, I can't hold in my groan. That little touch, that little trace of her tongue on me, she's too damn teasing. If I didn't need this from her, she'd already be bent over the bed, on all fours while I fuck her into oblivion.

She starts moving her hand up and down my shaft, slowly, very slowly, torturing me. I need more. Fuck, I need *more*.

She seems to notice because she leans down and takes me into her mouth. I arch off the bed, a loud moan escaping me. At first, she just sucks at the head, tenderly, before taking me deeper. I'm too big to fit in her whole mouth, and when I hit the back of her throat, she immediately gags and pulls away.

"I'm sorry," she immediately apologizes, her cheeks flushed.

"It's okay," I tell her. "I'll lead you."

She looks unsure, but nods, wrapping her luscious lips around me again. I wrap my fingers around the back of her head, leading her to take me deeper. When I hit the back of her throat once more, I keep her in place, not letting her pull away while her hand wraps around the rest of me, her fingers not touching.

I start thrusting into her mouth, and when she moans around me, it just spurs me on to move faster, and so I do, hitting the back of her throat with each thrust. I can feel her salivating around me, and it helps that there's no resistance as I slide in and out of her mouth.

After a few thrusts, she seems to have adjusted quite nicely because she takes me even deeper, clenching her tongue and palette together on me. I groan, throwing my head back and moving my hips faster.

"Fuck. I'm going to come." It's a warning. Let go now, or I'll come in your mouth.

But she doesn't leave me. Instead, she clamps onto me harder, forcing my orgasm to burst out of me and fill her mouth. She keeps her mouth closed, like she wants to keep it all in and swallow it all, but some still comes spilling onto her chin.

I see her throat bob. She swallowed it all.

"Good girl," I praise her because she deserves it, and she blushes, letting go of me with a pop. "Did you like that?"

She nods, and I wipe the remains of my orgasm off her chin.

"I want to do it again," she admits, surprising me. So, my girl likes giving blowjobs. Noted.

I smile but shake my head. "Not today, baby."

She pouts for a single moment before she nods in agreement.

"Now tell me, *stellina*," I start off, pulling my sweats back up my hips. "What suddenly got into you to do this?"

She avoids my eyes.

"Look at me when I'm talking to you," I demand, and immediately, her head snaps up, her eyes widening at my tone. "Now tell me the truth."

"I . . . I wanted to make it up to you," she says. "I hated myself after hurting you, and I just wanted to make you feel better."

"By giving me a blowjob?" I scoff. I can't believe my ears right now. "You must think so low of me if you think that you can just put your mouth around my cock, and I'll be okay with what you did."

Her eyes widen and she rushes to shake her head in panic. "It-it's not like that."

"Then what is it like?" I snap. "I told you I have feelings for you, and in return, you gave me a blowjob. What kind of sick transaction was this?"

"It's really not like that," she protests, her voice trembling. "I didn't do this to pay you back for liking me like you're thinking right now."

"Then why did you do it?" I question.

"Because I wanted to!" she exclaims. "I wanted to give you a first of mine."

Her first . . . her first blowjob.

Fuck, now I feel like an asshole.

"Even though we're engaged to get married, and you'll get my virginity anyway, I still wanted to give you this to show you how much you mean to me."

Fuck, that's really messed up, but if that shit doesn't make me hard.

Then she's scrambling off me, wiping away a stray tear that has fallen. Fuck, that hurts.

"I'm sorry if I made you think and feel that way," she apologizes, the sob in her voice tugging at my heartstrings.

"Baby . . ." I call out, but she's already out the door.

I run after her. I literally *sprint* so that I can get to her before she leaves the apartment entirely, and luckily, I manage to catch her just by the door, wrapping my hand around her wrist and pulling her to a stop.

"Let me go, Lucian."

"No. Not until we talk," I insist.

"Talk about what?" she bursts out, her lips trembling as she holds in her tears. "You told me that I think very low of you, but the truth is, you think the same of me. That's why you reacted the way you did and why you thought what you thought."

"No." I shake my head. "That's not true. I was just hurt, and so I was thinking the worst about everything. I don't think that way about you. I was just trying to justify myself for being a prick."

She just stares at me with unblinking eyes.

"I'm so sorry, baby."

Then she blinks, and she's wrapping her arms around me. I hug her back immediately, rubbing the back of her head like I always do.

"Never talk to me like that again. Never tell me to fuck off again. Let's just talk it out if it happens again. Please."

Her last word is a plead.

"I promise."

Chapter Twenty-One: Caterina

It's so warm.

I smile, snuggling further into the warmth. A pair of arms tighten around me, pulling me closer to the heat. I hum, rubbing my face on bare skin.

Wait. Bare skin?

My eyes open, and when they meet Lucian's, everything comes rushing back. Me showing up here, us having almost yet another fight, and then me spending the night at his place. Also . . . I gave him a blowjob. Lord, what possessed me to do that and tell him that I wanted to give him that first of mine, *and* I outright told him I'm a virgin.

Groaning internally, I curse under my breath. How embarrassing.

"What's going on in that pretty little head of yours, *stellina*?" Lucian's question pulls me out of my thoughts, and I look up at him again.

"Just . . . yesterday. What happened," I tell him the truth because there's no use in lying to him. He'll see right through me.

"You mean the fight," he starts off, and then a cheeky smile transforms his face. "Or when you gave me the best blowjob of my life?"

I blush so hard that it feels like my face is on fire.

"Ding, ding, ding. We have a winner." He applauds, knowing that he hit the spot right on.

"Don't tease me," I mumble, hiding my face in his chest.

"Okay, I won't, baby," he says, pulling my face away from

his chest so that he can look at me. "I promise."

"But . . ." I trail off, my cheeks becoming even redder at the mere thought of what I'm about to ask him.

"Yes, baby?"

"Was it really the best one of your life?" I blurt out. First, there's silence, and then, in a split second, the biggest smile appears on his face, and he nods.

"I don't tell lies, *stellina*," he assures me, running his fingers through my messy bed hair. "Now, I have a question for you."

I raise a brow at him, awaiting his question.

"Was that really your first time?"

I nod shyly.

"So, where did you learn to do that? How did you adapt to me so fast?" he asks, sounding truly curious.

"I read," I tell him honestly, his eyes flashing with surprise.

"You got that good at it by *reading*?" he questions in disbelief. I nod, and then his eyes suddenly darken. "And what other things have you read?"

"Hmm . . . basically everything." I'm surprised at how easily the truth about this topic comes out of me. "People think I'm super smart because I read, but I mostly just read erotica."

He bursts out laughing.

"Don't laugh. I'm serious," I whine, and he nods, shutting his mouth. "I've spent my whole life being sheltered, which means that I never got to do the things other girls my age were doing, and I didn't want to be completely clueless when it finally happened, so I read up on it. It turns out there are books *just* about that. There's no plot whatsoever. It's basically sex-ed."

"And I'm the first you've tried this with?" he asks once more.

I nod. "I'm glad I'm not half bad at it," I admit. When I was on my way here, it was all I could think about. That I couldn't screw up. That I had to make it good for him.

"Not half bad?" he exclaims in disbelief. "You're crazy."

The way he's shaking his head has me smiling. Then he's grabbing my hips, pulling me over on top of him.

"And from now on, you will not do *any* of the things you learnt with any other man but me," he says, his voice lowering to show me that he's being serious.

I immediately nod. It's not like I wanted to do it for other men anyway. Yesterday was the first. *He* was the first.

He smiles in satisfaction, leaning up to kiss me, but I pull away with a giggle, covering my mouth with my hand.

"Morning breath." I giggle, and he gasps.

"Are you saying my breath stinks?" he gasps out.

I shake my head. "No, not yours. Mine," I admit.

"You really think I care about something like that?" he questions, narrowing his eyes at me. "And FYI, you smell absolutely delectable in the morning." He nuzzles my neck with his nose, causing me to giggle.

"It tickles, Lucian," I say, trying to push him away, but he doesn't move. Of course he doesn't. He's like a boulder, and I'm an ant.

He nips at my skin, causing me to gasp both in surprise and pleasure. Who knew something so simple could cause an entire electric shock to go through me?

Then he places an open-mouthed kiss on the base of my neck, a shiver going through me when his tongue laps over the spot. He bites the spot once more, harder this time, and I can't help the moan that tumbles from my lips. I'm certain that will leave a mark, and surprisingly, I don't mind.

There's a part deep inside of me that *wants* him to mark me, for the whole world to see who I belong to.

When he pulls away, he stares at my neck in satisfaction, and I know. He did indeed leave a mark.

Now it's my turn.

Leaning down, I place a soft kiss on his jawline before

trailing my kisses down to his neck. He shudders when I kiss a certain spot, and I immediately bite down, soothing the sting with my tongue afterwards. It doesn't take much to mark him, and when I stare at it, I, too, am satisfied.

There's something inside me, something primal, that makes me want to mark his entire body.

Lucian stares up at me through half-lidded eyes, almost like he's drunk on pleasure.

I smile at him, moving the hair out of his face. I stare at him, *properly*.

He's so handsome. How did I not notice before? He's literally flawless, even with that cheekiness always present on his face and that mischief that lingers in his bright blue eyes.

"Why are you looking at me like that?" he asks, his voice husky.

I smile down at him. "You're so perfect," I tell him.

His eyes widen slightly before he shakes his head. "I'm not perfect," he protests. "I've done many things that've tainted me completely."

"I don't care," I say, honesty dripping from my every word. "You're mine now, and in my eyes, you're perfect. And that's enough for me."

"*Stellina*," he whispers, touching the side of my face. "How did I get so lucky?"

I smile, hiding my face in his chest. He makes me blush so much these days. It's weird.

"Baby, let's get married," he suddenly announces, and I laugh, lifting my head.

"We *are* getting married, you dummy." I laugh, but he shakes his head.

"No. I meant now," he says, his voice serious.

"Now? As in . . . right now?" I ask for clarification. He nods. "But . . . I know you've always wanted a big wedding."

"So? I don't care about that anymore. I don't even know

why I cared in the first place," he admits. "When Sandro married Havyn at city hall, it was admittedly very perfect. Just the two of them. No onlookers. No judgements. It was just about the two of them, and the entire hall was just filled with their love for one another. I want that. Not some big wedding with people who will judge us and gossip about us afterwards. I just want it to be you and me. Nothing can get more perfect than that."

There's so much raw sincerity in his words that it makes my heart clench in the most amazing way ever.

I feel tears at the back of my eyes, and I nod with a smile. "Okay," I agree. "Let's get married."

CHAPTER TWENTY-TWO: CATERINA

I'm getting married.
Right now.

It's almost unbelievable. But it's happening. And surprisingly, I can't be happier.

I never once thought my future husband would be Luciano Romano, but I'm glad that it is. I know he'll treat me right and make me happy, and I'll do the same for him. We *can* make this work.

I stare at myself in the mirror. I'm wearing a pure white satin dress that travels all the way down to my ankles. It dips in the cleavage area, but it covers up all the essential areas, thankfully. The dress is nothing extravagant, but it's just like me, well, who I really am. Simple. Just like Lucian likes, too.

To be honest, I was actually dreading that big wedding I thought we were going to have. It's true what he said earlier. People will just judge us and gossip about us afterwards. I hate the mere thought of that, but luckily, now I don't have to worry about that. All I have to worry about is showing up at city hall and getting married to Lucian, admittedly, my best friend, and now, my lover.

We haven't told anyone about this decision that we've made, and I prefer it that way. Knowing my family, they'd barge into city hall before we could even say our vows.

Oh, wait. Vows.

I didn't write any vows.

Oh, screw it. I'll wing it.

There was one person I told about this, though. My sister,

Alba. I couldn't keep it from her, not when she's the only person who's truly happy for me about this. Well, her and Mary, but I couldn't make her sneak out, not after what Father did to her the last time.

Alba stares at me, sniffling with real tears in her eyes.

"You look so beautiful, Cat," she says, breathing out. "The most beautiful bride ever."

"I'm not even in a real wedding dress." I laugh.

She shakes her head. "You don't need to have an extravagant dress, Cat. You're perfect just the way you are," she says. "*And* I know Luciano thinks the same way."

I can't help the blush that coats my cheeks. I want him to think that way. I want him to like me just the way I am.

"Oh, look at you blush," Alba teases. "You really . . . like him, don't you?"

My eyes lift to hers. The truth is, before, I never thought of Lucian as anyone more than just a family friend, given how much older he is than me, but slowly, he became my friend, too. And now that I thought about it, I've always been attracted to him. Whenever he looks at me, I blush. Whenever he touches me so gently, I feel butterflies in my stomach. Whenever he kisses me, I feel like melting into a puddle on the floor. I guess the truth is, I've always felt differently about him. I just didn't know that that was how I truly felt.

"I like him," I tell Alba.

She smiles. "I'm glad. If there's anyone who deserves to marry for love, it's you, Cat," she says. I walk to her, pulling her into a hug.

"Thank you." I breathe out. "For always being there for me, even when no one else was."

"I'll always be here for you, Cat. You're my little sister. Screw our parents and Viola."

We both laugh, and I pull away.

"Now, are you ready to get married?" she asks, and I nod.

I've never been more ready to be Mrs Luciano Romano.

She offers me her hand, and I take it, letting her lead me away.

We arrive at city hall shortly, and surprisingly, I'm not nervous. At all. If anything, I'm excited. This is my one chance at love, and I'm grabbing it with open arms. I'm choosing him, Lucian. To be mine and to be his. Forever.

"Your future husband pulled some strings so that you two wouldn't have to wait in line," Alba tells me, a teasing glint in her eyes as she calls him my future husband. I'm glad she approves of him. I don't know what I would've done if the one person I actually love didn't approve. Well, I guess, one of the people, because I'm planning on loving Lucian, and I know I'll be able to. He makes it so easy for me to fall for him. If I didn't know the true him, I'd be scared.

Alba leads me inside, and when we reach the doors of the hall where I'll be getting married, she squeezes my hand.

"You did well," is all she says to me before walking away to take a seat on one of the benches where she'll wait for us. Lucian and me.

I push open the doors and walk in, gasping at what I see. The entire hall is decorated in beautiful flowers with a red carpet in the walkway and rose petals scattered all over it. And in the centre of all of it, stands Lucian, my fiancé.

He did all of this . . . for me. So that I would still feel special on this day.

Tears spring to life in my eyes, but I try my best to hold them back. Alba worked hard on my makeup.

I walk down the red carpet, approaching the altar. Lucian looks absolutely handsome in his fitted grey suit that hugs his toned body perfectly. His hair is as messy as ever, just how I love it. Funnily, I think I would have been disappointed if he styled it. I want him just this way, the way he is.

His blue eyes are bright as I come to stand opposite him, not even trying to hide his happiness. That very happiness makes my heart feel so light.

"Shall we start?" the reverend asks, and Lucian nods, his eyes not leaving me.

The reverend starts, but I don't pay much attention to him, all my attention on my handsome husband-to-be.

I really like him, I quickly realise. I do want to marry him, and not just because of my previous engagement to a man twice my age anymore. No, now, I *want* to marry him. Just him.

"You may say your vows now," the reverend says to Lucian, who nods with a smile, his eyes still not leaving me. Good. I don't want to look at anyone but him, too.

"*Stellina*, my little star," he starts off, and I blink back a tear. "Since the moment we first met, you were it for me. That day, I swore that you would be mine someday. I'd protect you. I'd care for you. I'd love you. You mean the world to me, and I'm not just saying that. No, my world literally revolves around you. There isn't a day where you aren't on my mind, where I don't miss you, where I don't crave your attention. Even if you looked at me like you hated me, I never faltered. Because my feelings for you are true. I'm not perfect. Everyone knows that. I've made mistakes, I've hurt you, but never once did I mean to. You're my entire world, Caterina Russo, and from this moment on, I'll never let you go, not even if you beg me to. Because . . . because I love you."

I suck in a breath. He loves me. Lucian loves me.

"I promise to make you happy. I promise to make sure you always feel cared for. I promise to always shower you with affection. I promise to love you, not just in this life, but the afterlife, too."

Now I can't stop the tear that escapes my eye and rolls down my cheek. Thank goodness I convinced Alba against wearing foundation. Lucian is quick to wipe it away, his touch making my body heat up.

"Now, you may say your vows," the reverend tells me.

"To be honest, I didn't write any vows. I just told myself I'd wing it," I admit with a chuckle. "But now . . . I'm literally at a loss for words. I . . ."

Lucian grabs my hand, offering me a reassuring smile.

"I like you," I blurt out, and he blinks in surprise. "I really like you. I like you so much that it's a bit scary. But instead of being consumed by it, I've decided to embrace it. Because this . . . what I'm feeling . . . is something positive, and I can't think of a better person to feel this way for. I want to be with you forever. I won't beg for you to leave me. If anything, I'd beg for you to never let me go. I'll never leave you, either. I'll be by your side until the end. And then again, in the afterlife, because there's no one I'd rather be with in this life or the next. It's always been you, Lucian, and it'll always be you."

I take in a deep breath, feeling emotional.

"I plan on loving you. It's a promise, so just keep being yourself, and I'll keep falling deeper and deeper for you. That's all I need from you. Just be you, and I'll keep being me. And . . . I'll treat you good. I won't hurt you. I won't make you cry. I'll just make you happy every second of our marriage. That's my promise."

"Luciano Romano, do you take Caterina Russo to be your lawfully wedded wife?"

"I do."

"Caterina Russo — "

"I do!" I burst out, causing them both to laugh. I blush in embarrassment.

"Then, by the power vested in me, I now pronounce you husband and wife. You may kiss the bride."

Lucian wastes no time in engulfing me in his arms and pressing his lips to mine. When I feel the insistence of his lips,

I pull away. We can't get too carried away here, of all places.

When I look up at him with red cheeks, he's smiling at me.

This is it.

We're officially husband and wife.

Chapter Twenty-Three: Caterina

I stare down at the shiny ring on my finger.

It's not a huge rock, but rather a simple diamond encrusted with smaller diamonds around it. It might not be the most extravagant ring ever, but it's beautiful in all its simplicity. It's perfect for me.

I stare at my now husband, who's also looking at his simple silver wedding band, twirling it around his finger. He's staring at it with so much awe in his eyes, and I place my hand on top of his, wanting him to look at me like that.

He looks up at me, an immediate smile lighting up his face. "Are you happy?" he asks me, and I smile, nodding. "I am, too."

I can't take my eyes off him. He's so perfect, and all mine.

Unable to stop myself, I crawl onto his lap, my thighs on either side of his. We're in a limo with a private driver and the partition up, so I don't have to worry. His hands immediately go to my hips, squeezing my flesh. He doesn't say anything. He just stares at me with that soft look in his eyes and something else. He looks at me like I'm his entire world, just like he said in his vows.

Wrapping my arms around his neck, I lean forward. "I like you," I confess, and his eyes light up. I can't tell him I love him yet, because I don't, but I still want him to know how I *do* feel. I meant what I said in my vows. I'm going to fall in love with him, especially when he makes it so easy to love him.

"And I love you," he confesses. Then he nuzzles my nose with his own. "With all of me."

Don't cry. Don't cry. Don't cry, Caterina.

But apparently, my body didn't get the memo because I find myself sniffling, causing Lucian to frown in concern.

"What's wrong, baby?" he murmurs, wiping away a stray tear.

"I'm just so happy," I tell him. "You have no idea how much those words mean to me."

And it's true. My entire life, I've never felt like anyone truly loved me. Not even my mother, and it was clear before when she took my father's side over mine, even as it was obvious his decision would hurt me.

Closing the space between us, I kiss him. He moans, wrapping his arms around me and kissing me back with such ferocity that if I wasn't already on him, I'd be on the floor by now. I latch onto him like a leech, gripping the back of his thick neck with my hands, the hair there teasing my fingers.

"Wait, baby," he breathes out, breaking the kiss. "If we continue, I won't be able to control myself for much longer."

"Then don't," I murmur, tugging on his hair. He groans, leaning his head back against the seat.

Underneath me, I can feel how big and hard he is. Hard like a rock.

"We'll be arriving at the airport soon," he tells me, his words filled with warning. I merely smile, feeling oddly adventurous.

"Then I'll have to be quick then," is all I say before starting to unbuckle his belt. He groans in protest but doesn't stop me. I get off him, dropping to my knees in front of him. I know exactly what to do to relieve him, especially since he seemed to like it so much the last time I did it.

Reaching into his tight boxer briefs, I pull his length out, and it immediately springs up and stands up against his shirt.

"Baby . . ." He groans out, but I don't listen, leaning forward to lick the pre-cum off the head. He hisses, clearly very sensitive. And then I take him inside my mouth, as deep as I can, until the head hits the back of my throat. I moan around him, trying not to gag and wrapping my hands around the rest of him that couldn't fit.

I deepthroat him, clenching his length in between my tongue and my palette. He moans, throwing his head back, his eyes scrunched shut in pleasure. I suck and suck and suck while squeezing the rest of him with my hands. I start moving my mouth and tongue faster, practically sucking him dry.

"So good," he breathes out, his hand reaching out to grab onto my hair. "You take me so good, baby."

I moan at the praise, gasping when he pulls on my hair. His hips lift, and slowly he starts thrusting into my mouth, driving deeper and deeper until I can't help my gag. I don't let that stop me, though, sucking and squeezing him whilst letting him abuse my mouth, his thrusts becoming faster and faster.

And soon his thrusts become jerky, and I know. He's almost there.

He tries to pull out, giving me an out, but I clamp my mouth around him, not letting him go anywhere. He groans the loudest yet, and then hot thick spurts of cum erupt in my mouth. I swallow it all, not letting any of it escape like last time.

His taste might as well be an aphrodisiac. I'm addicted to it. In fact, I could suck and eat him every single day. Man, am I fucked up.

The cum keeps coming and coming, nearly choking me at one point. But then finally, he softens inside my mouth, and I pull away, letting him go with a pop.

Lucian releases a heavy breath, slumping into his seat and finally letting go of his death grip on my hair. When he looks down at me, I lick my lips, staring up at him with mischief in my eyes.

"You're a little vixen, aren't you?"

I merely smile, rising to my feet. And then suddenly, there's a knock on the tinted window.

"We've arrived, sir," the driver announces.

"Just in time," I say, reaching into my purse to top up my gloss while Lucian tucks himself back into his pants. When we're both presentable, Lucian signals the driver to open the door, and we climb out.

I gasp in surprise when I see the jet waiting for us on the pad.

"Is this yours?" I ask Lucian, turning to him.

He nods.

Wow. I mean, my family's rich, one of the richest families in Italy, but even we don't own a private jet. This is just yet another way the Romanos are on a completely different level from the rest.

Lucian places his hand on the small of my back and leads me to the jet. He helps me up the stairs, and even though I didn't need the help, I like having him take care of me. It's a first for me.

I gasp when we enter the jet. It's huge, with cream leather seats on each side, but what really intrigues me is the door at the far end. I wonder where that leads to.

"Can I get you two anything to drink?" the hostess appears by our side, a polite smile on her face. She's not checking Lucian out, good. I don't need to deal with jealousy so soon after we just got married.

"We're okay," he tells her when I shake my head at him. "We'll be at the back, so please knock before you enter."

"Noted, sir." She gives us a slight bow before walking away.

"What's at the back?" I ask Lucian, and he gives me a cheeky smile. Oh no, what does that mean?

He doesn't respond, just leads me to the back. When he

opens the golden door, I gasp in awe at what I see.

There's an entire bedroom and en-suite bathroom here. The bedroom has low golden lighting with white emitting lamps, and the king-sized bed is in the centre, pushed against the wall, with crisp white sheets and golden-covered pillows. There's even a big window on the other side, giving us a view of the clouds as we fly.

I rush to the bathroom, unable to contain my curiosity and excitement. The bathroom looks exactly how I thought it would. The walls are white with golden elements scattered all over, a huge tub in one corner, and a toilet and basin on the opposite side. There's another window by the tub, giving us the same view as the bedroom.

"What is all this?" I finally ask Lucian, staring at him with big eyes.

"It's a customized private jet," he tells me. "I wanted you to experience only the best luxury."

I purse my lips, touched by his words and actions.

"We'll be spending our wedding night here, and then we'll land in Bora Bora in the morning for the rest of our honey-moon."

Now I'm full-on sniffling, my lips forming a pout. This is so perfect. I launch myself at him, wrapping him in my arms and pressing my cheek against his chest. "Thank you," I breathe out. "This is all so perfect."

"It's just starting, baby," he murmurs into my hair. "I've got so much planned for you."

"So we're not just going to be locked up in the room all the time?" I ask, my voice teasing.

His eyebrows lift in surprise. "You vixen."

And then I'm up in the air with a squeal, and he literally throws me onto the bed. The soft mattress dips under my weight, and I sit up, leaning up on my elbows as I watch my husband.

When he reaches up to remove his tie, excitement creeps into my entire body. He slowly peels his blazer off and then his shirt. I suck in a breath at the sight of his bare chest. I've seen it before, obviously, but it still makes me breathless. Especially now that it's all mine.

He pulls down his pants and boxer briefs at the same time, leaving him completely stark naked in front of me.

"Come to me," I say, but he shakes his head.

"You've been a naughty girl, so I need to torture you a little," he murmurs, his voice husky. Torture? No matter what it is, with him, I know I'll enjoy it.

But what he does is not what I expect.

He wraps his own hand around his length and starts moving it up and down his shaft. I freeze, suddenly feeling envious of his hand. My own mouth was there just a while ago. I want it to be either my mouth or hand pleasuring him. I don't want his hand there.

Now I understand why he said it was going to be torture, because watching his hand pleasuring him instead of mine is torture.

He chuckles when I pout, doing my best to glare at him. He tilts his head to the side, as if he's taunting me, and starts pumping his cock, soft groans escaping his lips.

No! Only I should elicit those sounds from him.

Huffing, I can't believe I'm jealous of his hand.

I want to look away and pout like a child, but my eyes are glued to him, his hand. There's something dirty about watching him pleasure himself, especially since he's naked and I'm still fully clothed. I'm itching to undress, but I know it'll piss him off, so I refrain, squirming slightly.

Then Lucian suddenly stalks to me, cock in hand, and pulls me to the edge of the bed with his free hand and forces himself into my mouth. I gasp in surprise, but I don't pull away, enjoying the feeling of him inside my mouth.

He starts thrusting, and after a few more pumps and licks with my tongue, he's coming, spurting thick hot jets of cum into my mouth. It spills down my throat, and I swallow willingly, taking in as much as I can.

When I pull away, he's smirking down at me.

"You dirty girl," he murmurs. "You love my cock in your mouth, don't you? You love my cum inside you, don't you?"

All I can do is nod, staring up at him with big innocent eyes.

"Well, don't worry," he says, leaning down. "Because now you're going to feel my cum in a whole different part of you."

Chapter Twenty-Four: Caterina

I'm excited.

My excitement fills my body to the brim, and anticipation lights up my nerves.

I know exactly what's going to happen now, and I've never been more ready for it.

Lucian leans forward, helping me pull my dress over my head, then and tossing it carelessly aside. This now leaves me in only my panties, my sheer white lace panties. I didn't bother with a bra today, and when I see the hungry look in his eyes, I'm glad I didn't.

I love the way he's looking at me with such hunger. It makes me shiver with desire. He pushes me down onto the bed, bringing his face to my nether region and *sniffs* it. He literally sniffs it. *Me!*

"You smell so good." He moans, his warm breath hitting me.

"Lucian." I whimper, impatient.

"What do you want, baby?" he asks, his eyes meeting mine briefly.

I whine, not knowing what to say. What do I want? I want everything, his hands and mouth and tongue everywhere.

He seems to notice my indecision because he chuckles. "Don't worry, baby," he says. "I'm going to make you feel *real* good."

I know he will. Then he lowers my panties.

And then suddenly, his tongue flicks across my clit, causing me to gasp.

"You like?" he asks, his consideration for me causing tears to sting the back of my eyes. I'm not sure yet, the feeling foreign, but something in me tells me to nod, that I'll like it the more he does it, so I do, and he smiles.

Then he dips his head down and latches his lips onto my clit, suckling on the tender flesh. This time, a moan tumbles from my lips.

"T-that feels good," I stammer, my cheeks flushing.

I can feel his smirk against me, and then he moves further down to my hole, placing kisses on his way there, and then suddenly, he's sliding his tongue into me.

"Lucian!" I moan out loud, arching my back off the bed.

He grabs my hips, holding me in place, and then, just like that, he starts licking inside me, his tongue slightly ticklish.

My toes curl in pleasure, and I close my eyes shut when he slides his tongue out and then in again. In and out. In and out. In and out. Before much time, a foreign feeling builds up in the pit of my stomach, threatening me down there, and with a few quick licks and one singular suck, I find something shift inside me, my body tensing as the foreign feeling consumes me.

It takes a few moments for me to come down from my high, and when my eyes finally open, Lucian is hovering over me, licking the remnants of my release from his lips.

"Sweet," he says. "Just like I imagined."

He's imagined how I taste? The thought has that familiar warmth spreading throughout my lower body once more. Something must shift on my face, because he chuckles whilst smirking wickedly.

"You're just insatiable, aren't you?" He chuckles. "And I haven't even fucked you yet."

My insides unconsciously clench at the thought of having him inside me. He's big, so I know it'll hurt, especially for the first time, but I'm so wet down there, so slick that I bet he can just slide right in.

When he reaches down with his fingers, I know exactly what he's about to do, but I grab onto his wrist, shaking my head.

"I appreciate the prepping, but if I wait another moment to have you inside me, I might just die," I shamelessly admit. His eyes darken, lust shining in his blue orbs.

When he climbs off me, I whine, wanting to cry, but he quickly returns with a tiny bottle in his hand.

"I don't want to hurt you, so we're going to be using lube for the first time," he tells me before tipping the bottle over and pouring it onto his hand before wrapping that same hand around his shaft and coating himself with it. He uses such a generous amount that I'm almost certain it won't hurt at all.

When he's done, he carelessly tosses the closed bottle aside before climbing over me and situating himself between my legs. His thighs are so thick that I have to spread my legs far apart for him to come perfectly between my own.

"No condom?" I ask when he presses the head to my hole, and although I'm teasing, his eyes darken, and then suddenly, he slams into me, a cry of surprise leaving me.

"Lucian!" I gasp out, instinctively clenching around him.

"Condom?" he repeats, sounding appalled. He snaps his hips, and I whimper. "Why the fuck would I use a condom with you?"

It doesn't hurt as much as I thought it would, but although the lube helps a lot, it still stings a little.

"I was just . . . kidding," I force out, clenching my eyes closed.

"Don't tease me, *stellina*," he warns. "Because I'm planning on fucking you bare for the rest of our lives."

The thought that he sees us being together for the rest of our lives makes my heart swell, and I wrap myself around him, urging him on.

The moment the pain is gone, he knows immediately, and then he's pounding into me, fucking me into the mattress. His name leaves my lips in a helpless cry of pleasure, my head tipping back into the pillow.

"So good, baby," he grunts out. "You take my cock so good, baby."

I clench around him at the compliment, and he groans out loud, picking up the speed of his thrusts.

"You were made for me, *stellina*," he groans out, his length hitting a spot in me that has my eyes rolling to the back of my head. "I'll never fuck another pussy ever again. Only yours. Your perfect little cunt. The tightest and hottest pussy I've ever been in. The most perfect cunt ever."

I come at his words, squirting out my release without control. He groans, his thrusts becoming rougher and lacking the precision from before he chases his own release, and finally, with a loud roar, he comes, filling me with the warmth of his orgasm, and I instinctively clench around him, milking him for every last drop that he can give me.

"Fuck, I love you," he mutters, collapsing on top of me. My heart swells even further in my chest, and I keep my body wrapped around him, running my fingers through his hair as we both try to catch our breath.

I don't know how long we just lie there, my arms around him with him still nestled inside me before he finally lifts himself off me. He stares down at me for the longest time with a certain softness in his eyes.

"Why are you looking at me like that?" I shyly ask.

"Because you're perfect," he says. "Absolutely perfect for *me*."

I blush so hard that my face feels like it's on fire. He smiles at my reaction before groaning when I unconsciously clench around him again.

"Fuck, you feel so good," he says, dropping his face back

into my neck. "I want to stay buried inside you forever."

"Well, that can be arranged," I say, and he bursts out laughing.

"You're cute," he says, placing a kiss on the base of my neck. When he finally pulls out, I wince at the slight sting, and almost immediately, I feel so empty, my insides clenching on air.

He looks down with a groan, noticing the way my body reacts to his absence, and like he can't control himself, he quickly slides back into me before my hole closes completely, a satisfied moan escaping me when I feel how hard he is inside me again.

I've decided. I never want to stop fucking him or letting him fuck me. So when he thrusts into me hard and fast, I embrace it, pulling him even closer to me.

We lose ourselves in one another once again, and at this point, the thought that I may actually get pregnant from this runs through my mind, but I don't care. The realization hits me full-on.

I want to have his baby.

God, I want to have *all* of his babies.

And with that thought, I come again, not letting him go until he's fully emptied himself inside of me.

Chapter Twenty-Five: Luciano

I wake up to the most beautiful person right next to me. We're still in the jet, lying in the bed in the bedroom.

Soft breaths leave *stellina* as she sleeps, and I *almost* feel sorry for waking her, but what can I say? I'm fucking insatiable and officially obsessed with fucking her.

How did I go my entire life without this? If I knew being with her would feel like that, I'd never have fucked any girl before her. I'd have waited because she's most definitely worth the wait. It's really fucking amazing how compatible we are both in and out of the sheets. I've never felt more content in my life.

However, just as I want to climb over her and wake her up by sliding back into her tight heat, my phone rings from the bedside table. I groan, pick it up, and see Dante's name flashing on the screen.

Really? Why now? He fucking knows I'm on honeymoon right now.

I answer anyway, also knowing that he wouldn't call if it wasn't important.

"What is it?" I question without even greeting, speaking as softly as I can as to not wake Caterina up.

"Look, I know you're supposed to be on your honeymoon right now—"

"I am." I cut in, and he sighs into the call.

"Father had a heart attack."

I freeze.

"What?" I ask, sitting up in the bed. "What do you mean?"

122

"*A worker went to go and take him breakfast this morning when she found him passed out in the bed.*"

"And where is he now?"

"*The family doctor is by him, but it's not looking good. I called Alessandro, too.*"

If he called our other brother, it must *really* not be looking good. We don't have the best relationship with our father, but nonetheless, he's still our father.

I glance at Caterina's sleeping form.

As much as I want to enjoy this honeymoon with her, I know I need to go back to Italy to see my father. She'd force me to go back too if I didn't want to because, even though her father is also questionable, she knows the importance of family.

I slowly get out of bed and pull on my underwear before using the jet phone to tell the pilot to turn around and take us back to Italy.

I watch *stellina* as she sleeps with a smile on her face, not knowing about what's going on right now. When we get close, I'll wake her. I'll let her be at peace for now.

Caterina wakes up two hours later.

She yawns out loud, the smile still present on her face, but it quickly morphs into a frown when she sees the look on my face. She quickly shifts over to me and climbs onto my lap.

"What's wrong?" she immediately asks. "What happened?"

I place my hands on her hips, leaning back against the headboard.

"Talk to me, Lucian."

"My father had a heart attack," I inform her, and she gasps. "It doesn't look too good for him right now."

"Then why are we still here? We should —"

"I already told the pilot to turn the jet around," I tell her, already knowing what she was about to say. She nods before she reaches up and runs her fingers through my hair.

"And you?" she asks gently.

"What about me?"

"How are you feeling?" she whispers. "I know you don't have the best relationship with him, but he's still your father."

I knew she would understand.

"I don't know how I'm feeling," I admit. "I'm sort of going through all of this on autopilot."

"It's okay," she assures me just as I'm about to feel guilty about it, then places a soft kiss on my lips.

It's only now that I notice that she's still *completely* naked, her body on complete display for me.

"Will you ride me?"

She smiles and nods, lifting herself off me slightly to pull my boxers down my legs, and then she sits down onto me, sliding my entire length inside her in one move. I groan, dropping my head into her neck.

We don't speak, just our groans and moans filling the room as she rides me as if she's done this a million times before. It must be one of the things she's read about before, too. Either way, she's practically an expert, getting herself off by moving up and down on me and getting me off, too, by constantly clenching around me.

Neither of us lasts long, her coming first and me following soon after her.

Breathing heavily, we just remain like that, our foreheads against one another.

That was different, I realise.

That wasn't fucking right there. There was too much raw emotion mixed inside of it.

That was *making love*.

I've never made love to a girl before, but even that, not just the rough fucking, but the slow strokes and movements, it's perfect, too.

Everything is perfect with her.

"I love you," I tell her, and she wraps her arms around my neck, pulling my head into hers. She rubs my back up and down in a soothing manner, and I'm glad I have her by my side.

I don't know what I ever did without her as my wife.

I'm never letting her go. I'm going to keep her as mine.

Forever.

Chapter Twenty-Six: Caterina

We head straight to the Romano family house from the airport.

The drive there is silent. Neither Lucian nor I are talking, but I can still feel the anxiety rolling off him in waves. Yes, he says he doesn't really feel anything right now, but I think it's starting to catch up to him now that we're no longer thousands of feet in the air. Now reality is hitting him, and I have a feeling when he sees his father, it's only going to get worse.

Luckily, he listened when I insisted we get a driver to drive us, because he's clearly in no state to drive, not with that tight jaw and clenched fists. I reach over, wrapping my fingers around his fist and squeezing.

His head snaps to mine, surprise flashing in his eyes, almost like he didn't even know I was here. I don't doubt it. He's been in another place ever since we got off the jet.

We pull up to the house, and with one last squeeze, I let go of Lucian and get out of the car. The moment we're out of the car, though, he grabs my hand once more, like he needs this for me to ground him. I squeeze his hand again as we walk into the house and head to his father's bedroom.

When we reach the room, the door is open, and the air is ominous. Dante is standing on one side of the bed with Alessandro and his wife, whom I've never met before, on the opposite side, and lying in the bed is their father, his eyes closed, his breathing shallow, and his usual olive skin pale.

Lucian sucks in a breath upon seeing his father's state and squeezes my hand this time.

"Luciano." Alessandro is the first to greet him, while Dante just tips his head forward in acknowledgement.

"What happened?" Lucian asks, his voice sounding so unlike him. So rough and cold. "Was . . . was Father sick?"

They all share glances before shrugging.

"He's been living here alone for a while now, so there's no way of telling," Dante says.

"Don't blame yourself, Lucian," Alessandro cuts in, already sensing what was about to go through my husband's mind. "Even if you were still living here, he hides it well. You know that."

"Is he going to die?" Lucian blurts out.

Just at that moment, the doctor, dressed in uniform, steps out of the en-suite bathroom with a wet white cloth in his hands. He startles at the sight of Lucian, but he quickly bows his head, "Mr Romano."

"Is my father going to die?" he asks the doctor, who freezes.

"We don't know anything for sure yet," the doctor answers, his tone uneasy. Of course he's uneasy, being in the same room as such powerful people. "But I've been monitoring him, and I'll keep continuing to do so throughout the night."

"*Mi amore*," Alessandro calls out to his wife. "Why don't you go downstairs for a little while?"

She nods immediately, understanding that the brothers need some alone time with their father. Just as I'm about to join her, Lucian's grip on my hand tightens, keeping me to his side.

"Lucian . . ."

"Don't leave me," he whispers. "Please."

I share a glance with Alessandro's wife, who nods before disappearing down the hall.

"Luciano," Dante calls out, his voice stern.

"Don't," Lucian snaps. "My wife will stay by my side. I don't care what you think."

Dante scoffs but doesn't mention it again.

I'm not sure how long we just stand there, watching as the doctor tends to their father before Alessandro speaks up.

"It's late. Havyn has made dinner, so let's go downstairs."

Dante and Alessandro leave the room, but Lucian lingers, his eyes set on his father.

"Lucian," I whisper, using my free hand to cup his cheek. "It's okay. You can go. He'll still be here when you get back."

"How do you know?" he asks, his eyes serious.

"Because he waited for you when we were in the jet," I tell him, brushing the back of my hand along his cheek. "And he will wait for you again."

He swallows but nods and lets me lead him downstairs to where everyone's sitting at the table.

Lucian and I take two empty seats.

"Thank you, *mi amore*." Alessandro thanks his wife, Havyn, smiling softly at her. She sits down next to him, and everyone digs in.

I barely eat. My eyes are on Lucian the entire time, and just like that day before, I end up feeding him, because he only eats when it comes from my hands. We're in the middle of dinner when the doctor comes rushing down the stairs, his face crestfallen, and immediately, I know.

We all know.

He's gone.

Chapter Twenty-Seven: Caterina

L ucian lies sprawled all over me.

Since the news of his father's death, we've been spending every moment in bed, just lazing around and ordering in when we get hungry. We only part to eat, and the moment I'm done, he pushes me down onto my back and crawls on top of me, lying all over me with his face tucked into my neck.

He's heavy, but I don't tell him to move because I know he needs this. This affection, this love, and I'm going to give it to him, even when he rips my clothes off my body and thrusts inside me, not making love to me, but rather fucking me hard and fast until we both come so hard, we see stars.

I've lost count of the number of times we've been intimate in a matter of a week, but I don't mind, because not only does he need that closeness, I love feeling him inside me, too. I feel like he can't possibly get closer than when we're locked together and are one.

The funeral is today, and only the sons are allowed to attend, no outsiders, especially since they want to keep Gio Romano's death under wraps.

"Do you want me to come with you?" I ask him, running my fingers through his hair. I ask him this even though I've already made plans with Havyn for today since she'll be alone, too. I'll cancel if I have to if he needs me. But he shakes his head.

"This is something I need to do on my own, with my brothers."

I nod, placing a soft kiss on his forehead.

It may be wishful thinking, but I'm hoping that this entire ordeal brings the three of them together, because now they really only have each other. Besides their wives, of course.

I can't help but wonder how Dante is doing with all of this. Sure, he's a cold and emotionless man, but the thought remains. Maybe he's just putting on a façade, and at this time, when his brothers aren't around, he's all alone with no one to comfort him.

It's sad.

Eventually, the time comes for Lucian to leave, and with one last emotional quickie, he does leave just as Havyn appears at the door.

"Come on in," I tell her, letting her in. "So, what do you want to do today?"

"Well, I was actually hoping we could go shopping for something," she says, her voice hesitant.

"Sure?" I say in confusion at her tone.

"A test," she suddenly says. "A *pregnancy* test."

"You're pregnant?" I burst out, but she quickly quiets me down.

"I don't know," she answers. "We've been trying, and I haven't gotten my period, so I just figured I'd take a test just in case."

I nod. That makes sense.

"Let's go then," I say, and we're off.

When we get to the store that sells just about anything and everything, we stop by the aisle where the pregnancy tests are and contemplate which one to buy.

"Isn't the most expensive one the most accurate?" I ask her as she taps her chin in thought, and then she nods.

"Yeah, I think so."

She grabs seven, yes, seven, of the pregnancy tests and then just a few extra from random brands to make sure whether she's really pregnant or not. She's going to need to drink a lot of water for this.

We don't get weird looks when we pay, and I quickly realise it's because of the rings on our fingers. As soon as we reach my home, she drinks up about a litre of water before heading to the bathroom.

She takes quite a while, but just as I start to get worried, she calls out my name. I walk to the bathroom where the door is already open, and step inside, my eyes finding Havyn's figure as she stares at the multiple pregnancy tests laid out on the vanity.

When I take another step forward, I see it.

Two little lines.

On every test stick.

"You're pregnant!" I exclaim, pulling her into an unexpected hug. She sniffles onto my shoulder, and I freeze. "Are . . . are you not happy?"

"I'm so happy," she says with a shake of her head. "I just can't believe it."

"You deserve it," I tell her.

We dispose of all the pregnancy tests and toss them in the garbage disposal on the ground floor of the building before returning to the apartment. Just as we sit down to relax, she digs into her bag and produces yet another pregnancy test.

"You not sure yet?" I tease because she had at least ten positive tests back there. She shakes her head before holding it out to me.

"It's for you."

"Me?" I ask, and she nods. "But I'm not pregnant. Trust me."

"With the way you two are going on, you will be soon," she says, a mischievous glint in her eye, and almost immediately, my face warms up.

"How long were you actually outside the door?" I ask.

"Long enough," she answers, and I groan in

embarrassment. "Don't be embarrassed. Alessandro is the same. Very insatiable. I think it's a Romano thing."

I find myself laughing through my embarrassment before nodding, making a mental note to hide the test away. I don't want Lucian to get any ideas ahead of time.

Havyn and I end up spending the rest of the day just talking, her mostly gushing about her husband with hearts in her eyes, and I'm sure I look the same when I talk about Lucian.

We're both just so lovesick, and it makes us laugh, but we embrace it.

"Honestly, I never thought I'd fall for someone like Lucian," I tell her. "Not because there's anything wrong with him. It's just . . . we've known each other for so long, it almost seemed impossible to see him as something more than a friend."

"But you do," she says, and I nod.

"I . . . I think I love him," I say it out loud for the first time. She smiles, especially since she knows about our situation.

"You don't have to force it, Caterina," she tells me, reaching out to squeeze my hand reassuringly. "But love is a beautiful thing, and if you truly do love him, you should tell him. I think that's what he needs most from you right now."

I let her words sink in, and at that very moment, the front door opens, and our husbands come walking in.

"Where's Dante?" I can't help but ask, worrying about their lonely brother.

"He has work," Alessandro answers with a shrug.

Lucian doesn't say anything. He just heads my way immediately and pulls me up and into his arms. He nuzzles my neck with his nose, breathing in deeply.

"I missed you," he says. "So much."

I place a kiss on the crown of his head, wrapping my hand around the back of his neck.

"We should get going, too," Havyn says as she stands,

sending me an excited look. Oh, she's definitely happy to be pregnant. I can't help but feel a twinge of envy.

Lucian and I haven't even been married that long, but I already want to have his child, and I think this feeling has intensified because he just lost someone so close to him. A baby would be a surprise, and a blessing, and it would definitely lift his spirits.

I'm going to give that to him, I decide.

I'm going to try hard, and then I'll give it to him.

I'll give him everything his heart needs and desires.

Chapter Twenty-Eight: Luciano

My phone ringing rouses me from my sleep.

Stellina groans from beside me, burying her face in my neck. I blindly reach over to the bedside table, grabbing my phone and answering it without even bothering to look at who it is.

Only an idiot would dare call me this early in the morning.

"What?" I snap into the call, and then I hear a familiar chuckle. Yep, definitely an idiot. "What do you want, Dante?"

"You still into watching illegal underground fighting?"

My eyes flutter open. Illegal underground fighting?

Fuck, I can't remember the last time I went to one. Those were fun times.

"Unless you're inviting me to one, you better hang the fuck up right now," I warn him, and he chuckles once more.

"It's a good thing I'm inviting you then," he says.

"Really?" I ask. "What's the catch?"

"Just didn't feel like going out and meeting a stranger tonight," he says, and I know he's shrugging without even seeing him. That's strange, especially for him because he's *always* up for taking a stranger to a hotel and fucking their brains out.

My immediate answer is yes, especially since I haven't heard or seen much from him since the funeral, and I admit, I do feel bad because Alessandro has Havyn, and I have Caterina. He has no one but his daily booty calls to keep his bed warm at night, and that doesn't involve any emotion. It's just all so cold and clinical.

"Cool. I'll see you tonight then." Then he hangs up. Always

to the point and then bye-bye without even saying the word goodbye.

"Who was that?" Caterina murmurs into my neck, her voice still sleepy.

"Dante," I answer. She hums, and I pull her closer, running my fingers through her locks.

I know how she feels about Dante even though she didn't tell me. She feels sorry for him, and I completely understand. He's completely alone right now with no one by his side who truly cares about him. Sure, he has me and Sandro, but he wouldn't come to us if he's lonely or having a tough time. He's very independent, especially after being so dependent on our father in the past, and he likes to do things and work things out on his own.

It also doesn't help that he refuses to let anyone in, not since . . .

I shake that thought off. I shouldn't be thinking about her, especially after what she did to him.

The truth is, I'm the only one who knows the truth about what happened between Dante and his first love, since I was there to witness it firsthand, and I've never shared it with anyone, not only because it's not my place but because it really scarred him. It's hard when you love someone so much and they just discard you like nothing but used toilet paper.

I don't know what I'd do if Caterina did to me what Izabella did to Dante.

Fuck, her name went through my head. That's a bad sign. A bad omen. *She* is.

When *stellina* finally wakes up properly, I tell her that I'm going out with Dante tonight.

"Can I come with?" she asks.

"It's not really that safe . . ." I trail off. A woman shouldn't be in a place like that, especially not a woman like her.

"But you'll be there to protect me," she points out. "Please.

I'm really curious."

I hesitate.

"I'll behave, I promise. I won't stray from you. I'll stick to you like glue," she begs, and when she adds that pout of hers, I'm putty in her hands.

"Fine." I give in. She cheers in triumph before placing sloppy kisses all over my face, muttering about ten *thank you's* in the process.

Then she's up from the bed and rushes into the bathroom to pee.

I lay back in the bed, thinking about us.

We've been married for about two months now, and it's been amazing. I can't wait to come home to her, and I love waking up next to her with her in my arms. I don't know how I ever survived saying goodbye to her before because now I can't live without her.

Yes, I'm aware I'm whipped, but I don't even care. I love her, and that's the most beautiful thing ever.

Then suddenly, I hear a loud gasp come from inside the bathroom, and I'm quick on my feet and by the door, but it's locked.

"What happened? Are you okay?" I rush out, banging on the door.

"I'm fine," comes out in her soft voice. "Just tripped over my feet." She ends it off with an awkward chuckle, and I release a breath of relief.

She takes quite a long while in the bathroom before unlocking and opening the door. When she steps out, I pull her into my arms, placing a kiss atop her head.

"You okay, my baby?" I murmur, my voice soft. She sighs before looking up at me with a look in her eyes that I don't quite understand. I've never seen that look before.

Then she's leaning up and pressing her lips to mine.

I immediately tighten her in my arms, flicking my tongue

across her bottom lip. She opens for me so quickly and so willingly that I can't help but thrust my hips into hers, causing her to moan.

Fuck, I'm already hard and dying to be inside her.

Picking her up, I let her wrap her arms and legs around me before carrying her to the bed and laying her softly down on the sheets before crawling over her. I run my eyes down her body, her body clad in a lacy bra and matching panties.

We usually sleep naked, but on the off occasion that we don't fuck, she insists on sleeping in her underwear.

I grab onto the sides of her panties and pull until a ripping sound fills the air. She doesn't even gasp like she used to at the beginning, just rolls her eyes at me with a knowing smile on her face.

Her bra hooks at the front, so I quickly unclasp it, setting her breasts free. I immediately grab each one in my hands. They fit fitting perfectly in my palms. She moans, lifting herself up to kiss me again.

I moan into her mouth, thrusting my tongue into her wet cavern and licking my way into the back of her throat. She wraps her legs around my waist, grinding up against me until I groan.

"Fuck me, please," she begs against my lips. "I need you inside me now, please."

Now, how can I tell her no when she asks so nicely?

Directing the head of my cock at her entrance, I push forward, sliding simply the head inside her. I can already feel the precum leaking into her.

"More, please."

She's so impatient and needy for *me* that I can barely take it.

Putting her out of her misery, I push all the way in to the hilt in one single thrust, and a loud moan leaves her mouth, which I swallow with my tongue.

I ravage her mouth as well as her pussy, snapping my hips repeatedly, my balls hitting the crease of her ass.

Moan after moan leaves both of us, our lips separating and my face falling into her neck when she clenches around me. Fuck, she loves doing that, and as much as I love it, too, I want to make this last.

So I pull out completely, causing her to whine in protest.

"Turn over," I order.

She does so quickly, lying flat on her stomach.

"On all fours."

She listens, holding herself up using her hands and knees with her ass sticking up in the air.

We've never done this before, and I love that even though this position is very vulnerable for her, she's still so eager and does what I say without hesitation. Because she *trusts* me.

Angling myself at her entrance, I push in, a moan of relief escaping both of us. She loves me being inside of her as much as I love being inside her. I know.

I fuck her fast and hard, pounding her into the mattress, the headboard hitting the wall with every thrust. She pushes back, meeting me thrust for thrust until I go deeper inside of her than I've ever been before.

"Lucian," she whines, seeking her release. Wanting to make this even better for her, I reach down and start stimulating her clit.

With a few strokes of my fingers and my dick, she comes with a loud scream, arching her back into me.

I pull her up so that her back is against my front and start thrusting upwards, fondling one breast in my hand whilst digging my other hand's fingers into her right hip, knowing that it'll leave a bruise. A mark, and by the way she's moaning, I know she likes it.

Soon, after a few sloppy thrusts, I find my release, pushing so deep inside her that I'm certain I'm spilling into her womb, and this fact has her coming again with the loudest moan yet, my name leaving her lips.

She slumps back against me as we both breathe heavily, coming down from our highs.

"Like that," she mumbles, resting her head on my shoulder, her eyes closed with exhaustion, and I chuckle, reaching up to move her sweaty hair from her face and tucking it behind her ear.

When I start to pull out, she unconsciously clenches around me, and she whimpers.

Yep. We're definitely doing that again.

Chapter Twenty-Nine: Luciano

The venue is filled to the brim with people.

Nothing new, and just like I thought, Dante got us regular seats, albeit in the front row, as in places like this, we like to keep a low profile. It's just a part of the fun.

We take our seats just as the first fight is about to begin. I'm in the middle with Dante to my right and *stellina* to my left. She's been brimming with excitement ever since we left the apartment, and it shows on her face, her big doe eyes sparkling with interest and curiosity.

The first fight is quite boring, between a big muscular guy and a tall lean guy who clearly doesn't know how to use his agility properly and ends up getting knocked out in three seconds flat.

Next, though, is an interesting fight.

A girl comes up to the ring, wearing trainers, a full black tracksuit that covers her entire body, and her natural ebony curls hanging loosely. This is the first time I'm seeing her here, and I've been here a lot.

The crowd seems to know her, though, chanting her fighter's name, Black Slayer, repeatedly, not even caring for her opponent, who's easily twice her size even with her medium height.

When the fight starts, I gasp out loud. She's good, really good, moving fast and swiftly and landing hit after hit against her opponent.

Stellina stares at her in awe as she beats up her opponent, making me smile. If I knew she'd like this so much, I'd have brought her a long time ago. Even though it's not a great place for a girl like her to be, I love the look on her face.

She's not the only one completely enamoured by this girl, though, because when I turn my head to Dante, he's staring at her with such intensity in his eyes. And . . . something else. Something I know too well.

Desire.

This is the first time I've seen him react to a girl like this in a very long time.

When she knocks out her opponent and the fight's over, she disappears out back where I know all the other players are. Dante is quick to rise to his feet, his eyes slightly widening when he sees me watching him.

"You good?" I ask him, my lips curled up into a smirk. He freezes, obviously realizing he was caught.

"You should go after her," my wife tells him, an encouraging smile on her face.

He hesitates, and it's quite obvious that this is something out of his comfort zone, and maybe he's even a little . . . nervous.

"Go, Dante," I urge him on. "I won't tease you."

I glance at *stellina,* making a point of showing him how much love I have for her and that I'm not embarrassed by it. That it's okay for him to *feel* something.

With one look at us, he's gone, following her. I can only hope she hasn't completely left the venue yet.

"What do you think is going to happen there?" *stellina* asks me.

I smile. "I think my brother might just find love again."

Chapter Thirty: Caterina

I can't believe what I'm seeing.
What I'm looking at.

Two little pink lines.

Positive.

I'm *pregnant*.

It feels surreal. Yes, I've been wanting this for a while now, and every time Lucian and I've had sex, I always had that at the back of my mind afterwards. That it was just yet another chance I might conceive. But now that it's actually happening, I feel weird. I don't know how I'm feeling. I'm excited but nervous at the same time.

It's been about a week since I took the first test, and I've been taking one each day since then, wanting to be sure before I tell Lucian.

Looking down, I place a hand on my flat stomach.

Soon, I'll swell up with my baby. Lucian's and my baby. *Our* baby.

Okay, the reality sets in, and I'm squealing.

I need to call Havyn.

Dialling her number, I press the call logo, and she answers after merely a few rings.

"Havyn!" I exclaim, my excitement overtaking my nerves.

"*Someone sounds lively,*" she comments. "*Something I should know?*"

"Can we meet?" I ask instead of answering her question.

"*Of course. Where?*"

"The . . . city hospital."

"The hospital? Why the hospital? Are you sick?"

I chuckle.

"I wouldn't be so lively, as you put it, if I was sick, now would I?" I tease.

She releases a loud breath of relief.

"Okay, I'll meet you there in an hour."

We bid goodbye before hanging up to get ready.

I take a quick shower before slipping into a pretty pink flowery sundress and a pair of flat sandals. Now that I'm pregnant, there's no way I'm wearing heels anymore, not even wedges. I can't afford to fall, no matter how early I am in the pregnancy.

"And where are you going looking so pretty?" Lucian startles me when he appears in the doorway. "Not dressing up for another guy, are you?"

I know he's teasing, but there's still a possessive undertone in his voice that has me shaking my head and walking to him.

I wrap my arms around his waist, smiling up at him. "I'm going out with Havyn," I inform him. His eyes flash with surprise.

"You two getting along?" he asks, and I nod.

"We kind of bonded while you guys were at the funeral," I admit, expecting him to wince or something, but surprisingly, he just smiles.

"I'm glad. I want you to have a friend, and I trust Havyn," he says.

Leaning up, I place my lips onto his for a quick kiss.

"I love you," he murmurs against my lips. I tense up slightly.

I love him, too, I just haven't said it yet. I tell myself it's because I'm waiting for the perfect moment, but the truth is, I'm scared. Not of him, but because I've never told anyone I love them before.

I'll get there eventually. I will.

"I'll get going," I tell him, placing another kiss on his cheek, this time before walking out.

When I get to the hospital, Havyn is already waiting at the entrance for me, pacing up and down like she can't help herself.

"Havyn," I call out, grabbing her attention.

"Oh, thank god," she breathes out, grabbing my arms. "Are you okay?"

"I'm fine," I assure her with a slight eyeroll. "Let's go inside."

We take the elevator up to the doctor's rooms, and when we stop in front of a gynaecologist's room, Havyn's eyebrows furrow in confusion.

"I already have a gynae," she says in confusion, but I just chuckle and walk in, heading for the front desk.

"Caterina Romano, appointment for twelve PM."

The receptionist scrolls on her computer for a few moments before telling me to have a seat and that the doctor will be ready for me soon.

"What the hell is going on?" Havyn hisses.

"Well . . ." I trail off.

She must see something on my face because she gasps. "You're pregnant?"

"I think so," I answer.

"Oh my god," she says, gasping out loud. "We're pregnant at the same time. I mean, I'm further ahead than you, but our babies are going to be besties!"

She's so excited, enough for the two of us.

I look down at her stomach. She's already showing a little, especially since she's so short and petite.

"Mrs Romano," the doctor calls out. I got a female gynae-cologist since we all know Lucian would freak out if a man

144

was fiddling with the goods down there. Havyn did the same, too, not wanting to anger her husband.

"So, how are we today?" Dr Gallo asks, smiling at me.

"Good," I answer uneasily. "A little nervous, but mostly excited."

"Good, so have you taken a test?"

"Five, to be exact," I say with a nod, and she chuckles.

"Okay, so we're just going to do one more test, just to be sure," she informs me, and I nod.

She makes me pee in a cup before sticking a stick inside it.

"Pink means pregnant," she tells me beforehand, and then slowly, she lifts the stick in the air.

Even though I've gotten five positives before this, I clench my eyes tightly shut in anticipation and fear. I was so excited when I saw that last positive, but what if this one, the one test that *really* counts, comes up negative?

A few long moments pass by before... Havyn shouts, "Pink!"

My eyes snap open, and indeed, the stick is pink. A bright pink.

I'm pregnant.

I'm *actually* pregnant.

Havyn hugs me tightly, jumping up and down as I process everything.

Looking down at my belly once more, I smile.

There's a human being growing in there.

Our human being.

Now I just have to tell Lucian the good news.

Chapter Thirty-One: Luciano

My wife's late.

It's been all of *nine* hours since she left.

She said she was going out with Havyn, so I wasn't worried. I *wasn't . . .* but now I am.

Where is she?

Then there's banging on the door, and I run to open it, disappointment filling me when I see Sandro standing there instead of *stellina*.

"Where the fuck is my wife?" he bursts out.

"What do you mean where's *your* wife?" I bite out. "Where is *my* wife?"

We're both heaving and staring at one another in confusion and anger.

"Where the *fuck* are our wives?" he questions in realization.

They're both missing.

Within two seconds flat, I have Dante on the phone.

"I'm busy —"

"Caterina and Havyn are missing." I cut him off. There's a single moment of silence before he speaks again.

"Give me fifteen."

And then he hangs up.

"Havyn's phone is off," Sandro says when he fails to contact his wife. I don't call *stellina*, though. Dante will find them. Dante will find *her*.

Within ten minutes, Dante calls me back.

"The Dungeon."

The Dungeon? *Again?*

She promised she'd never go there again.

Oh, now I'm pissed.

Sandro takes the wheel when he sees how visibly angry I am, and when we pull up in front of the club, I stalk over to the bouncer.

"Where the fuck is my wife?" I snap, glaring up at him. His eyes widen when he realises who I am.

"In the VIP section," he answers, pointing inside, and I storm in, Sandro hot on my heels.

The VIP section in this place can barely be called a *VIP* section when all it has are a few torn-up couches and a makeshift bar on the side.

I trudge up the stairs, my eyes immediately finding my wife sitting on one of the couches, huddled up against Havyn, flutes with what I'm assuming is orange juice, although they might have added vodka or something to it.

I hate to admit it, but she looks like she's having fun, and I *almost* feel bad about what I'm about to do.

"Caterina Romano!" I yell out, everyone going silent in the VIP section. Even the music playing in this secluded space stops playing.

Her head snaps to mine, her eyes widening. I stalk over to her, my face stern.

"What the fuck are you doing?" I snap, but when she flinches at my tone, I find the need to apologize and whisper to her that it's okay and that I'm not mad at her, even though I am.

Sandro pulls his own wife aside, and I'm left alone with *stellina*, who stares up at me with guilty eyes.

"What are you doing here, *stellina*?" I soften my voice, not wanting to scare her. The last thing I need is for my wife to be scared of me. Anyone but her.

"I was just trying to have some fun," she whispers, her doe-brown eyes pulling me in. So, feeling my heart soften, I lean down in front of her, placing my hands on her knees.

"Have you been drinking?" I ask her, but she shakes her head vehemently, looking horrified.

"No! I'd never drink now! How can I drink when I'm—" She stops talking abruptly, pursing her lips together.

"What are you talking about? Why can't you drink now?" I ask her in confusion. She stares at me through big eyes, appearing to be contemplating something.

"You're pregnant, for fucks sake!" I hear my brother yell out. *Caterina's* eyes flitter to them.

"I didn't drink!" Havyn yells out, throwing her arms up in the air. "We were just here to celebrate, for goodness sake!"

"Celebrate what?" he questions.

"Our pregnancies!"

And then her eyes widen, as if she just realised she let something slip.

My brain is too quick for her, though. My head snaps to Caterina. "*Our* pregnancies?"

She bites her lower lip.

"I'm sorry!" Havyn exclaims, tears filling her eyes. "I didn't mean to. It just came out."

"Caterina," I call out, my voice stern but gentle. "Talk to me, baby."

Upon hearing me call her that, she collapses into my arms, wrapping herself around me like she always loves to do.

I don't speak anymore, just gently rubbing her back up and down. "It's okay, baby," I murmur into her hair. "It's okay. We're okay."

She nods with a sniffle before pulling back slightly to look at me. And then she says the words that has my entire world stopping. "I'm pregnant."

I freeze. I literally freeze.

She takes it the wrong way, her lips trembling as they form a pout and her eyes welling up with tears.

"Do you not like it?" she whimpers. "Do you not want a baby? With me?"

"No, baby," I soothe. "That's not it. I'm . . . of course I want a baby with you. I want all the babies in the world with you."

"You do?" she sniffles, and I nod.

Cupping the side of her face, I say, "I'm so happy."

A smile lifts her lips.

"You've just made me the happiest man on the planet." Then I reach down to touch her stomach. "I can't wait for you to swell up with my baby. I can't wait to start a family with you."

Her eyes glisten with happiness.

"I love you," she says. I suck in a breath, her arms tightening around me. "I love you so much, Luciano Romano."

She loves me.

Unable to stop myself and not caring that we're in a public place, I lean forward and capture her lips with mine.

"I love you." Kiss. "I love you." Kiss. "I love you so fucking much."

She smiles into the kiss, muttering those three words again.

I love her, and she loves me.

I can't be happier.

"My star."

Epilogue: Luciano

"We're never having sex *ever* again!"

I can't find it in me to laugh at the death glare she's sending me, or at least trying to send me, but all she looks like is an adorable little bunny with those doe eyes of hers.

I wince when she tightens her death grip on my hand, practically crushing my hand in hers.

"Don't you dare complain," she warns me. "Childbirth is a thousand times more painful."

I stare at my wife, sweat trickling down her face and her hair soaked in it.

"You're doing so well, *stellina*," I say, trying to soothe her, but she just glares at me.

"I see the head!" the doctor suddenly says. "I'm going to need you to push now, Mrs Romano."

A pained cry leaves my wife's mouth as she pushes.

"All right, good job," the doctor praises. If only she knew my wife has a praise kink. "Push again."

Caterina's face scrunches up as she pushes once more.

"Okay, you're doing so well. Now give me one big final push."

Caterina *screams* as she gives her final push, and then suddenly, a soft cry fills the room.

She collapses back onto the bed, and I watch in awe as the doctor holds *our* baby in her arms, wrapping *our* baby with a blanket.

It might be old-fashioned, but *stellina* and I decided to keep the baby's gender a secret from ourselves so only the doctor knew, but now as I stare at our baby, tears well up in my eyes.

It's a *boy*.

A little prince. Who will carry on the Romano line.

"*Stellina*," I call out softly, taking our baby boy from the doctor. "Look. It's our *son*."

Her tired eyes flutter open, and a smile lifts her lips.

"A boy?" she repeats, and I nod.

"We made a boy." I sniffle, not even caring about my reputation at this point. "A handsome little prince."

She holds out her tired arms, not too tired to hold the baby she carried for nine long months and just gave birth to.

"Oh, my little baby boy," she breathes out in disbelief, a tear falling from her eye. "You're so handsome. And all mine."

"He's *ours*, baby." I smile at her, placing a hand on her shoulder.

She smiles up at me with glistening eyes, with tears of joy, and I can't help but lean down and place a single kiss on her lips.

"I love you," I mumble against her skin.

"And I love you," she says, and then she decides to tease me. "Almost as much as I love our son."

I laugh, shaking my head at her.

"I wouldn't expect anything less," I say, rubbing her head up and down. "You're a natural mom, after all."

She smiles and then, as if she can control it, her eyes slowly flutter closed, and I take our son from her, cradling his little body in my arms.

Caterina sleeps for a solid eight hours, and when she wakes up, the first thing she does is look for our son. She releases a breath in relief when she sees me sitting in the chair next to her bed, holding him in my arms.

I give him to her immediately, knowing that she needs this

now. To be with her son. To hold him. Especially after she slept so long.

"What do you want to name him?" I ask her, leaning forward towards them.

"Lorenzo," she answers immediately. "Enzo for short. Meaning prince."

"You've done your research," I note, and she smiles shyly.

"I had an inkling." She simply shrugs with a teasing smile.

Grabbing her hand, I link our fingers together and brush a kiss along her knuckles.

"I love it."

Her smile just brightens even further, and then she looks at our son, taking his tiny hand into her free one.

"You hear that, little prince?" she coos. "Your name is Enzo because just like the name means, you're a prince."

Then there's a knock on the door, Sandro's head popping in. I laugh, gesturing for him and Havyn, who is carrying their month-old daughter, Aurora, to come in, and surprisingly, Dante trudges in after them.

"Oh my," Havyn gasps out. "It's a boy."

"Lorenzo," I quickly say, glancing at *stellina*, who smiles at me. "Enzo, for short."

"Cute." She gushes.

Dante just stands aside awkwardly, but I see the slight smile tugging at his lips. Caterina notices immediately.

"Enzo," she grabs his little hand and lifts it up into a wave. "Say hi to your uncles. Uncle Sandro and Uncle Dante."

Surprise flashes in Dante's eyes, especially when my wife smiles up at him and asks, "Want to hold him?"

His eyes widen like he's horrified, and he shakes his head. "I've never held a baby before. I don't want to drop him or hurt him," he admits, staring at his own arm muscles that could probably crush our baby in one go.

"Next time, when he's bigger, then," she says before

bringing her attention back to Enzo.

As I look at everyone in the room, I realise. This is my family. My wife, my sister-in-law, and my two brothers. My forever family.

And now my little boy, whose eyes are fluttering open for the first time, revealing a pair of baby blues identical to mine.

He's definitely going to be a heartbreaker in his days.

ABOUT THE AUTHOR

I have lived my entire life Cape town, South Africa where my life is run by 2 furbabies, a husky named Saskya and a cat named Stripey. I'm a hopeless romantic who dreams of having the kind of love I read and write in books. Coffee and music are my writing companions. When not writing, I like creating art with my hands and paint tiny canvases. My sister has never let me live down THE oven incident. In my own defense, she asked me to turn the oven on, she did not ask me to set the temperature. My only secret, my obsessions are known by those who know me best, but even they don't know about my solo karaoke sessions.